7.3.17

WITHDRAWN

Get **more** out of libraries

Please return or renew this item by the last date shown.
You can renew online at www.hants.gov.uk/library

Or by phoning 0300 555 1387

14 ₸₋ᵤ₆

Hampshire
County Council

Dedicated to the memories of Misty, Oscar and Charlie.
I was their human, and their willing servant.

SHEILA NORTON

OLIVER

THE CAT WHO SAVED CHRISTMAS

EBURY
PRESS

1 3 5 7 9 10 8 6 4 2

Ebury Press, an imprint of Ebury Publishing
20 Vauxhall Bridge Road,
London SW1V 2SA

Penguin
Random House
UK

Ebury Press is part of the Penguin Random House group of companies
whose addresses can be found at global.penguinrandomhouse.com

First published in 2015 by Ebury Press
This edition published in 2016

www.penguin.co.uk

A CIP catalogue record for this book is available from the British Library

ISBN 9781785033551

Printed and bound in Great Britain by Clays Ltd, St Ives PLC

Penguin Random House is committed to a sustainable future
for our business, our readers and our planet. This book is made
from Forest Stewardship Council® certified paper.

CHAPTER ONE

The worst night of my entire nine lives started with some leftover fish. You might think that was a bit strange, little kitten. After all, we cats all love fish, don't we, and I often used to get leftovers, living in a pub where they made something called bar meals for the people who came in. It wasn't actually the fish I had that night that was the problem. It was what came afterwards, when I'd gone back to my favourite chair by the fireplace and fallen asleep.

Now, stop jumping around trying to catch that fly, if you want me to tell you the story. It's a long story for a little kitten like you, and a bit frightening in places, but you might learn something from it if you settle down and pay attention. That's better.

Where was I? Oh yes. Asleep on my chair. Well, I woke up very suddenly when it was dark outside – and there was a horrible smell in the pub, and something tickling my nose and throat. I knew straight away it was smoke, because sometimes when my human, George, lit the fire in the bar to make it nice and cosy on a cold evening, it gave off the same kind of smell. But when he did that, the smoke went up the chimney, not into the room like this. I blinked for a few minutes, trying to see what was going on. Of course, my night vision is normally excellent, but the smoke was making my eyes sore. Within a few minutes I was starting to cough and choke because it had started

3

going down my throat too, when I did the normal stretching and yawning thing we have to do when we wake up. And then I saw them – big orange flames leaping up the curtains, and sparks flying onto the nearby chairs.

I yowled in fright. At least, I tried to, but all that came out was a pathetic squeaky noise and another bout of coughing. I jumped out of my chair, heading for the staircase to the upstairs rooms, where I knew George would be asleep in the big bedroom overlooking the garden. Luckily he always left his door open, in case I woke up in the night and decided he might appreciate my company on the bed. So I darted straight in and jumped on him, pawing at his face to wake him up. I was trying my best to meow loudly in his ear at the same time, and despite all the coughs and splutters, it seemed to do the trick because he sat up in bed, gasping in surprise.

'Oliver!' he said, sounding a bit annoyed. He usually only called me by my full name when I'd been naughty. 'What on earth . . .?'

And then he must have smelt the smoke, because he leapt out of bed, shouting, 'Oh my God! Fire! Fire!'

There were only the two of us in the building so I couldn't understand who he was shouting to, but I was very relieved he'd woken up. He grabbed his mobile phone off the bedside table and his dressing-gown off the hook behind the door, and I ran ahead of him along the landing and back down the stairs. I was frightened to see that the flames had spread and were now working their way up the wooden banisters, spitting sparks and billowing more black smoke. I bounded down those stairs as if there were a couple of Dobermans after me.

'Outside, Ollie, quick!' George shouted, beginning to cough like me.

As he unlocked the main door to the bar the cold outside air rushed in and it was as if the whole place suddenly erupted. The crash, as the staircase collapsed, was so terrible, I shot out of that door and kept running, right across the car park and under a bush at the other side, next to the road. I could see George, in his stripy pyjamas, running out with his dressing-gown still in his hand, dropping it while he stabbed at the mobile phone and shouted into it: 'Fire! The Forester's Arms! The pub's on fire!'

I stayed under the bush, shaking with fear, watching the fire work its way up to the roof of the pub, watching as the wood store next to the kitchen went up with a 'whoosh'. Then the flames spread to the fence, and then they were licking around some kind of big drums lined up behind the village hall next door. And then there was a sudden loud 'boom' that made me jump out of my skin, and the fire seemed to roll itself into a ball of orange that lit up the whole sky.

For a minute I was frozen with terror. I thought it was the end of at least one of my lives, for sure. There were people running out of their houses, shouting, looking for George, putting his dressing-gown and blankets round him, as if it wasn't hot enough with all those flames. And just to add to the horror of it all, at that moment two massive fire engines came tearing down the road towards us, sirens screaming, and turned into the car park right next to the bush where I was cowering. Well, I knew I should have stayed to make sure George was all right, but my cat instinct told me I needed to get out of there as fast as I could. It wasn't my proudest moment, deserting my human and my home. But I'm afraid I scarpered.

When I finally stopped running, I was in the middle of the woods across the road. I looked back through the trees but I couldn't see the pub anymore, or even the flames. The trees were very tall and very close together here, and I realised I'd gone further into the woods than I'd ever been before. My heart was still pounding like mad from the shock, as well as from running so fast. I put my head on one side to listen carefully, but all I could hear at first was the sound of the wind blowing through the trees and an owl hooting in the distance. It was really cold, and I felt so sorry for myself, all alone there in the woods. All I wanted was to be back in my chair, curled up on my nice comfy cushion, asleep and dreaming my favourite dream about chasing mice. But I was too scared to go back. And then, as I was still standing there listening to the wind and the owl, and shivering and shaking like a leaf, there was suddenly another loud 'boom' from the direction of the pub. All the birds who had been asleep in the trees flew up in the air together, squawking with fright, and once again my cat instinct took over. I shot up the nearest tree, right up to one of the highest branches, and clung on for dear life as the wind rocked me back and forth.

You'll find when you grow up to be a bigger cat that the best way to deal with a stressful situation is to get out of danger quickly and then go to sleep. I've heard humans talking sometimes about 'not being able to sleep'. They say it happens when they're worried about something. Fortunately this condition is unknown within the cat community. I was so worn out from the terrible shock I'd had, I could hardly keep my eyes open once I was safely snuggled down on that branch. There were no more booming noises, and although from the top of the tree I could see a rather scary red glow in the sky, far away in the direction of my poor pub, it gradually got fainter and fainter. The wind dropped slightly and the movement of my branch became more gentle, reminding me of the times I'd dozed on the old rocking chair in the back room of the pub. I closed my eyes and dreamed George had come to find me and was carrying me home.

When I woke up it was light, and there were birds singing. I stood up and had a good stretch, completely forgetting where I was, and almost fell out of the tree. Luckily my claws were out instantly, so that I was suspended for a moment, clinging to the underside of the branch until I managed to right myself. I gave myself a little shake, and automatically started to wash myself to show any birds who might have been watching, sniggering at my misfortune, that I wasn't the least bit embarrassed or bothered how silly I might have looked. And then, in mid-wash, I glanced down, and saw it at the bottom of the tree. A fox.

Little kitten, I don't suppose you're old enough to have met a fox yet, so let me explain. If you think dogs are scary, you haven't seen anything yet. Foxes don't even have humans in charge of them like dogs are supposed to. They're one of our worst enemies, almost as dangerous as cars. At least cars normally stay on roads, so we know how to avoid getting attacked by them. But foxes sneak up on you. They get into gardens and even walk down the street, just like we do, and if they see you they'll chase you with their horrible big smirking mouth open showing their horrible sharp teeth. There's only one way to get away from them – run up the nearest tree. So although, as you can probably imagine, my fur was standing on end at the sight of this snarling vicious creature staring up at me from the ground below, I knew I was in the best place. He couldn't get me. I was so relieved about this that I actually started showing off to him a bit, arching my back at him and hissing and spitting – until I nearly overbalanced again and decided no amount of bravado was worth falling out of the tree and landing on top of him.

I sat back down on my branch, stretched out my paws and let my head hang over the edge so that I could keep one eye on the fox. I could tell he was getting annoyed about not being able to climb up and get me. He was pacing up and down at the bottom of the tree, walking round its trunk one way and then back round the other. And the whole time he was staring up at me, with a look on his nasty face like I can feel on my own when George puts a nice plate of food down for me. I shuddered to myself. If I put one paw out of place on that branch, I'd be his dinner. To my relief, after what seemed like hours of this walking round and round, the stupid fox must have got tired. He lay down, curled up like a little puppy dog, and fell asleep. I was safe for a while. The best plan of action would be to have another little nap myself.

It wasn't until I woke up, and saw him still there at the bottom of the tree, that I realised three things, all at once. One: I'd had no breakfast and was now feeling very, very hungry. Two: I didn't know which way was home anymore. I'd lost its scent, and there was no more red glow or smoke in the sky to tell me. And three: until that fox moved, I was stuck. If I tried to jump into another tree, he'd just follow me. I couldn't get back down to the ground until he went away. And he didn't look like giving up any time soon.

I thought about George, and my chair, and the warmth of the pub, and my food dish being filled up with lovely chicken or fish, and I couldn't help it, little kitten. Even big grown-up cats cry sometimes. I sat on my branch and mewed pitifully to myself as the fox licked his lips and dribbled revoltingly beneath me. And I wondered if I'd ever see George or my home again.

CHAPTER
TWO

It was getting colder, with a dusky sort of look in the sky, by the time I heard a new sound coming towards me. I sat very still, my ears up, listening carefully. It was like music, but different. The fox sat up too, and was looking around him nervously, and then he suddenly loped off, giving me an angry backward glance as he went. The sound was coming closer. I waited, my head on one side, trying to remember where I'd heard it before. And then it came back to me. Whistling! That's what they called it. Humans did it by putting their mouths into a funny shape and pushing their breath out. It made a kind of tune that wasn't always very pretty. Finally I heard the footsteps of the whistling human, treading on the dead leaves on the ground. And there he was, just a few trees away from me, walking quite quickly. If I didn't shout now, he'd be out of earshot – humans don't have very good hearing, you know. But was he someone I could trust? I wasn't good at trusting humans, especially strange male ones – but that's a story for another time. Well, this time I didn't have a lot of choice, and I made a quick decision. If he was doing that whistling thing, he probably wasn't in a bad mood. I'd noticed before that they did it when they were cheerful. So I stood up again on my branch and yowled as loudly as my little lungs would let me.

He stopped whistling, stood still just a little way from my tree and stared around him. Just a little further on, the fox was standing looking back too, but I hoped he wouldn't risk coming back while the man was there. I don't think foxes like humans. There are stories in cat folklore – and they might be made up, of course – that humans long ago used to ride around on horses, blowing horns and using dogs to *hunt* foxes. It sounds a bit unlikely, but I wouldn't put anything past some humans. Anyway, there I was, crying and screaming out to get this man's attention, and there he stood, looking up, down, and all around him with a puzzled expression on his face. Like I say, they don't have very good hearing. But luckily, eventually he caught sight of me and it was the way he said, 'Well, hello, up there' in such a nice friendly way, that made me relax a bit and think perhaps I'd be able to trust him.

In fact he carried on talking to me as he approached my tree, smiling up at me and calling me a 'nice puss' and asking whether I'd got stuck up the tree. Although I was very glad he was being so friendly, I felt a little bit patronised then, as I'm sure you can imagine. Stuck up the tree, indeed! Anyone would think I was an inexperienced little kitten like you. I wanted to tell him that if he'd only use his eyes, he'd notice there was a great big nasty snarling fox hiding in the undergrowth, watching us from a safe distance. Otherwise I'd have got down from that tree on my own, no trouble at all, thank you very much!

But I must admit, he was a pretty good tree climber himself. He was a fairly young, lean human and made good use of his front paws to swing himself up through the branches. He kept saying things like 'All right, good puss, sit tight, don't panic.' Then as soon as he was close enough, he reached out and grabbed me with such a sudden movement I nearly toppled off the branch with fright. I let him hold onto me going down again, which was a bit awkward for both of us, but I wanted to let the fox – if he was still watching – see that I now had a protector. When we were nearly at the bottom I jumped down, but stayed by the human's feet, giving him a little display of gratitude, rubbing myself on his legs and purring. He looked down at me, a bemused expression on his face.

'OK, you can run off home now, puss!'

I continued my rubbing and purring. He watched me for a bit longer.

'What is it, then? Are you lost?'

Hooray! He'd got the message. I purred a bit louder. He picked me up again and looked at the little disc on my collar.

'Oliver,' he read out. 'And no address, just a phone number.' He got one of those mobile phone things out of his pocket, tapped it and sighed. 'No signal here. Well, maybe I'd better take you home with me, Oliver, and give you some milk or something and then I can try . . .'

The mention of milk had reminded me of how hungry and thirsty I was, and I practically jumped into his arms this time when he bent to pick me up again. I'd decided I liked him. Perhaps he was a good one, like George. But then, to my horror, he picked up a bag he'd left by the tree trunk and pushed me into it, quite clumsily, head-first so that my tail nearly got caught in the zip as he did it up.

I yowled my head off in protest. So much for trusting him! But as I felt him lift the bag up, he was talking to me through the flap.

'Sorry about this, Oliver. You'll be safer in the rucksack on my back, see, while I walk home with you. Otherwise I'm frightened you'll jump out of my arms and run off when we get to the road, and there'll be cars, and it'll be dangerous. All right, all right!' he said as I carried on complaining. Well, honestly! It was *so* undignified, to say nothing of bringing back some terrible memories for me. 'It won't be for long. Just try and sit still like a good puss.'

So I had to bump along in that bag as he strode off, whistling again. The bag was smelly and uncomfortable, with some bits of twigs at the bottom of it, and the walk seemed to take forever. Eventually I could tell from the sound of traffic that we were out of the woods, and then it wasn't long before I heard him unlocking a door, closing it behind me and calling out, as he put my bag down gently on the floor:

'Hello? Are you home, Nick?'

Then there was someone else's voice – a young female by the sound of it:

'Oh! You were quick! I've only just got in from the shop. Did you manage to get some firewood?'

'No. Sorry.' I felt him lift the bag again. 'Look what I found instead.' He started to undo the zip – I braced myself to jump out and hide in a corner somewhere until I'd made sure it was safe here, wherever I was. But then he stopped and asked: 'Are all the doors and windows closed?'

'Of course they are! It's freezing out! Why, what on earth have you got there?'

And the bag was opened, and I made a dive for it – straight up the curtains at the nearest window.

'A cat!' squealed the female person. 'Where did it come from, Daniel? Why have you brought it home?'

'He was stuck up a tree! I got him down, and he wouldn't leave me. I think he must be lost. He's got a name tag on, with a phone number, but I didn't have any signal, so I thought I'd better bring him home.'

'Poor little thing!' she said, looking up at me now, having apparently got over the shock of seeing me run up her curtains. 'He looks scared stiff. Come on, kitty cat – what's his name, Dan?'

'Oliver. He's very friendly. Come on down, Oliver,' he added in that nice kind voice I liked. 'I'll get you some milk.'

Great. I was gasping for a drink. I jumped back down and followed him into a little kitchen where he poured me out a nice dish of milk, which I lapped up immediately and licked the dish clean.

'I reckon he's hungry,' he said. 'I don't know how long he'd been stuck up that tree. Can we give him something to eat, Nicky?'

The girl started emptying tins out of a shopping bag onto the kitchen counter.

'I've got some sardines here,' she said doubtfully. Sardines! Yes – result! I immediately started winding myself round her legs, purring for all I was worth. 'But they were supposed to be for lunch,' she added quietly.

17

'We can have something else, can't we? You've got baked beans there. I'll phone his owner as soon as he's eaten. We won't have to keep on feeding him.'

They were looking at each other with worried faces. I wondered what the problem was. I just wanted those sardines!

'OK,' the girl called Nicky finally agreed. She started opening the tin. The smell made me feel faint with hunger and longing. 'Here you go, Oliver.' She put the dish down on the floor and I fell on it. 'Good grief, Dan, he must be *starving*!' she added, laughing. 'Fair enough, his need's even greater than ours.'

Out of the corner of my eye, while I wolfed down the food, I saw him put his arm round her and give her a kiss. That was good. I'd seen people sitting together in the pub doing that, and it usually meant they were happy.

'I'm sorry about the firewood,' he was saying. 'I'll go out again later.'

'No, it's five o'clock now and it's dark already. Leave it till tomorrow and I'll come with you. We can carry more, together. I just don't think we can afford to put the heating on.'

'I know. How much was the shopping this time?'

'Not as bad as last week. The butcher gave me some cheap mince, and I got special offers on tea bags and butter.'

'Well done.' He gave her another kiss. 'We'll manage, Nick. If we can get through the winter, things will get better.'

And they stood like that, arms round each other, watching me till I'd finished eating. I had the impression they liked me but at the same time, wanted me to go home as soon as possible. And sure enough, the minute I'd finished the last morsel, Daniel picked me up and called out the number on my identity disc, while Nicky punched the numbers into her phone.

'There's no reply,' she said after a while.

'OK. Well, the owner's probably just gone out somewhere. Looking for their cat, probably!' he added, but Nicky didn't laugh.

'We can't keep him, Dan,' she said.

'I know. Of course I know that.' He stroked me, and I gave him a little purr. I wanted to go back to George, obviously, but I was feeling full and safe and warm now, and could easily have fallen asleep right there in Daniel's arms. It had been a terrible time, what with the fox, and the trauma of the fire . . .

The fire! I meowed and twitched my tail anxiously as it all came back to me. Poor George! My poor pub. Did I even *have* a home to go back to now? I wanted to explain to nice Daniel and Nicky that the number on my disc might belong to a phone that was lying in a burnt-up wreck of a building where nobody could live anymore.

'He still seems a bit distressed,' Nicky commented, and she gave my head a little stroke. 'Perhaps you're right, he might have been lost for ages. Although he doesn't look too thin.'

I took that as a compliment.

'Let's just try the phone number again later on,' Daniel said. 'I'm sure someone will be out looking for him. He's such a lovely cat and he looks well cared-for.'

I *knew* he was a human I could trust. He had good taste in cats. I was purring to myself happily as he put me down on a sofa, and I dozed off into a nice peaceful sleep.

CHAPTER
THREE

It was a different voice that woke me up – a strange male voice. I was instantly on high alert, ears up, muscles tense, ready to run. The voice sounded friendly enough, but you can never be too sure.

'I know who that is!' The voice belonged to another male, a large one with a bristly face. I didn't like the look of him. I gave him a warning growl as he came closer, but he just laughed. 'It's Ollie, the pub cat from the Forester's Arms. You know Ollie, don't you? Everyone in the village knows Ollie.'

Daniel and Nicky exchanged a sad kind of look. 'We never go there,' Daniel said.

'Oh. No, well, I suppose you haven't lived here very long. Well, he belongs to George, the landlord. Blimey, I suppose he's got nowhere to go, now. I take it you've seen what's happened to the pub?'

'Oh, yes, of course!' Nicky gasped. 'The fire.'

'Yes, it's pretty badly damaged, isn't it?' said Daniel. 'And the village hall doesn't look much better.'

'Well, the fire brigade managed to put it out before the hall burned down completely, but you're right, the pub and the hall will both be out of action for God knows how long.' He stroked his bristly chin, looking at me seriously. 'I wonder why old George didn't take the cat with him when he left.'

Left? *Left*? I sat up straighter, unable to believe what I was hearing. George wouldn't *leave*, without me!

'Where's he gone?' Daniel asked.

'To stay with his sister in London. Poor chap hasn't got any other family, see. His sister's offered to put him up till the repair work's done. I reckon that'll be the best part of a year. The insurance will have to pay out, of course, but you know how long that can take.'

'How awful for him. Losing his home *and* his livelihood,' Nicky said, looking upset.

'And his cat,' the big man said, nodding at me. 'We ought to let him know you've found him.'

'We've tried, twice now. The number's on his disc. No reply,' Daniel said.

'What number is it? Let me have a look.' The big man reached out for me, and I yowled in fright and jumped off the sofa, running to hide behind the curtains. They all laughed. I didn't really see what was funny. I was beginning to recognise this man as one of a group who came into the pub fairly often. They were always quite noisy together, drinking a lot of beer and playing something called dominoes that made them shout and laugh a lot. I always tried to stay clear of them. He seemed all right now, but like I've said, I don't take chances with male humans until I'm sure of them.

'Let me pick him up, Martin,' Daniel said. 'He seems to have got used to me. I found him stuck up a tree in Tunny Woods.' He lifted me up and showed him my identity disc.

'That's the pub number,' Martin said at once. 'No good to you now! You'll be needing George's mobile. I've got it – I call him on that when it's about the dominoes team matches.' He sighed as he got his own phone out of his pocket and started tapping it. 'We won't have anywhere to hold *those* for a while. We'd booked a table for our Christmas meal there, too. Ah well, that's not important in the scheme of things, I suppose . . .' He broke off suddenly, then shouted into the phone: 'George? It's Martin here, from the dominoes team. Sorry about the fire and everything, mate. How're you doing?'

Daniel had put me back down on the sofa and Nicky was sitting next to me, stroking me, as we all listened to Martin telling George that I'd been found, safe and well, up the top of a tree. I felt so upset, knowing that my human, my best friend in the whole world, was on the other end of that phone, but I couldn't see him or even hear him. I cried a few sad little meows and Nicky stroked me harder, saying 'Ah, poor Oliver.' I told myself that at least I'd fallen on my paws with her and Daniel, when I could have ended up as a fox's dinner, so I really shouldn't feel too sorry for myself.

'Would you guys be happy to hang onto the cat till he can sort something out?' Martin said when he'd finally said goodbye to George.

Nicky and Daniel were looking at each other anxiously.

'How long's that likely to be?' Daniel said. 'Only I'm not being funny, but I thought George would be coming straight round to collect him.'

So did I. I mean, they seemed nice people, and they seemed to like me, but I missed George, and it was horrible to think he might not *want* me back. Had I upset him in some way? I'd done my best, hadn't I, going upstairs to wake him up and warn him about the fire. I couldn't have done much more.

'No,' Martin was saying. 'He's in a bit of a pickle, by the sound of it. His sister's being very good, putting him up and everything. But she lives on a main road in a busy part of London, apparently, and George says the cat's not used to heavy traffic. He'd be worried all the time about him getting out and getting run over. So he was wondering whether anyone in the village would be able to look after Oliver for him.'

I'd given a little squawk of alarm at the thought of the heavy traffic. It was true, cars frightened me. There weren't usually too many on the roads in the village, but there was a big loud main road a bit further down the hill from the pub. I'd heard people calling it a bypass and saying the village was much more peaceful since it had been built – but it scared the life out of me and I stayed right away from it.

'Not only that,' Martin went on, 'but his sister suffers from allergies. Cat hair's the worst thing.'

Oh, allergies – yes, I'd heard about this before. A lady who came into the pub once, started sneezing really badly and when she saw me, she made a fuss in between sneezes, saying cats shouldn't be allowed in pubs because of our hair and people's *allergies*. George was very nice to her about it, saying how sorry he was about her sneezing, but he explained the pub was my home and he couldn't expect me to stay outside, and perhaps if she'd like to sit in the other bar (where the meals were served and I wasn't allowed), she'd be all right. But she went off with a cross face and never came back.

'Oh dear,' said Nicky, and she looked at Daniel again, and he looked back at her, and both their mouths were turned down. Nicky was still stroking me, so I knew she still liked me, but there seemed to be some kind of problem here.

'We can't keep him,' Daniel said, looking upset. 'It's just, to be quite honest . . .' He went a bit red and didn't seem to want to go on.

'We can't afford to feed him,' Nicky blurted out. 'I'm sorry. It's embarrassing to admit it, but we can hardly afford to feed ourselves. The rent . . . and our fares . . .'

'Oh, right, of course, I understand,' Martin said. He sort of shifted from one paw to the other, the way humans do when they feel awkward. 'Everyone's hard up these days, aren't they, what with the bloody government, bloody banks, economy being what it is . . .' He tailed off, and then added quickly, 'Well, look, I could always take him back next door with me, instead.'

I stiffened again, ready to run up the curtains. No *way* was I going home with him. I didn't trust him yet. His voice was too loud, his face was too red and bristly, and he had very big front paws. I looked at nice Nicky and meowed my distress to her, but she didn't seem to be taking any notice.

'Are you sure?' she said. 'But you and Sarah have got the two kids to feed, and . . . well, isn't it a bit soon after Sooty?'

Sooty? Who was Sooty, and what did he have to do with it? I meowed again, my anxiety increasing.

Martin's face seemed to turn sad for a minute. Then he gave a little shrug and I saw him making an effort to smile again.

'I think it'll actually *help* the children to get over Sooty. Having another cat around could be exactly the right thing. We're going to get another one of our own, of course. We just haven't really had time to think about it yet.'

So Sooty was a cat, and it sounded like something had happened to him. And Martin sounded upset about it. I stopped meowing and gave him another glance. If he'd had a cat already, and missed him, surely he couldn't be all bad.

'Anyway, we've got more space next door, and a garden,' he went on, and this time his voice sounded more cheerful again. 'And the kids would play with him'.

I felt sorry that something had happened to this Sooty cat, of course, but if I'm really honest, I was relieved that there wasn't going to be another cat next door if I went there. The thing is, little kitten, *some* male cats can be really funny about what they call their *territory*. They go around spraying everywhere to mark their boundaries and get quite aggressive if any other cat crosses into their area, even if it's by accident. That's how a lot of fights start. I could never see the point of it – I prefer a quiet life, myself.

'Well,' Nicky was saying now, and she was still stroking me, still looking at me sadly, making me think she'd like me to stay really. 'It might be better for Oliver, too, because we're both out at work all day and he might get lonely. Are you absolutely sure it'll be OK with Sarah?'

'Of course it will. Sarah's a soft touch with animals.'

That was good to hear, too. I was beginning to think it might be OK to go with Martin after all. But I still flinched when he went to pick me up, and this time it was Nicky who laughed.

'Martin won't hurt you, Oliver,' she said, and she picked me up instead. 'Come on, I'll carry you in next door, shall I? You'll like Sarah. And the children.'

Children. Kitten-humans. That'd be interesting. I often used to watch some playing outside the pub, on the village green. Perhaps they'd play with me. At least that'd make the time go more quickly until George could come back for me.

The house next door was completely different from Nicky and Daniel's. Not that I'd had much time to explore theirs, but the living room was tiny, and the kitchen where I ate my food was not much bigger than the broom cupboard back at the pub. And when I'd been hanging onto the top of their curtains, I'd looked for a garden, but there wasn't one: just a little bit of paving with one of those washing lines that goes round and round in the wind. When Nicky carried me into Martin and Sarah's house, I could see the garden straight away, through the big glass doors at the end of the lounge. There was lots of nice grass, and bushes – places for hiding – and even some swings like the ones they had on the village green for the children. There were two little girls playing in the garden, wrapped up in coats and boots, chasing each other around. It looked like fun and I quite fancied joining in. But Nicky sat down with me on her lap while Martin explained all about me to Sarah.

'Oh, poor Oliver!' Sarah said when she'd heard the whole story about George and the pub and the sister with the allergies. She was a smiley, cuddly-looking female, with pretty long golden hair, and she kept smiling at me. 'Of *course* he can stay with us. The children will love him, and I'm sure you're right, it'll help us all get over Sooty.'

'Well, if there's any problem, we'll take him back. We'll manage somehow,' Nicky said anxiously. 'I'd *love* to look after him, if only . . .'

She looked so sad at not being able to afford my dinners, I felt really upset for her. I gave her a little lick on her hand and rubbed my face against hers.

'He's really taken to you, hasn't he?' Sarah said. 'Tell you what – we could kind of share him, couldn't we? Till George comes back? I mean, we'll feed him here, of course, it's no trouble, as I only do a bit of freelance work so I'm here most of the day. But I bet he'll still come next door to you for extra cuddles.'

Well, that seemed to cheer Nicky up, and it did me, too. Yes, I certainly seemed to have fallen on my paws! Not one new foster-home, but two. Neither of them were going to be as good as being back with George in the pub, of course. But I just had to be a big brave cat and make the best of it. There were a lot of cats worse off than me.

And I'd been through a lot worse myself, in fact, when I was a very small kitten, even younger than you. But as I've said already, that's another story. I might tell you one day, even though it still makes me shiver to think about it. But right now, little kitten, it's getting late, and getting dark, and I think we both need to go back for our dinners. I'll tell you some more tomorrow.

CHAPTER
FOUR

CHAPTER
FOUR

Hello again. You're awake early, aren't you? Couldn't sleep? Huh, I remember feeling like that sometimes when I was a younger cat – on nice bright mornings like this, when there were birds to chase and flies to jump around after. Now, there aren't enough hours in the day for all the cat-naps I need.

Oh, it's because you're excited to hear the rest of my story, is it? Well, I warn you, it might take a long while and you'll probably get fed up before the end of it and want to be off dancing around in the sunshine again. What it is to be young!

All right, where did I get up to yesterday? Ah yes – Martin and Sarah's house. I slept well there, that first night. Sarah made me up a lovely comfy bed in Sooty's old basket, with soft blankets and some kind of furry toy from one of the children to keep me company. Of course, you know what it's like, don't you? I didn't often sleep there after the first night. No matter how comfy a bed is, we cats like to find different places to sleep. There was an armchair in their lounge with a big thick velvety cushion on, that I was particularly fond of.

Anyway, let me tell you about the children. They were two small females, called Grace and Rose. Grace was bigger than Rose. She giggled a lot and moved around very quickly. She got so excited when Sarah introduced me to her,

I thought she was going to run up the curtains. Rose was different – quiet and not so happy looking. I could see why. She had a damaged front paw. It was wrapped up in a kind of hard case that looked like a bandage, and she had to wear something they called a sling, like a harness round her neck, to keep it in place. I felt sorry for her and gave her some extra licks and rubs, but although one minute she was smiling as if she was pleased to meet me, she suddenly burst into tears and started saying 'Sooty! Sooty!' over and over while she cried. I didn't like to think I'd upset her. I ran off and hid under a chair.

'Don't worry, Oliver,' Sarah said kindly, bending down under the chair to talk to me. 'It's not your fault. Rose is still upset about losing her other cat.'

Well, after a little while she did stop crying, and the two girls played with me nicely indoors with a ball and an empty cardboard box. Yes, I know you might think I was a bit old for that kind of stuff, but we cats never grow out of the cardboard box thing. It's just *so* much fun, I never get tired of it! While we were playing, I could hear Martin and Sarah talking quietly in the kitchen. They probably thought none of us could hear, but perhaps they forgot what sharp ears we cats have.

'I hope we're doing the right thing,' Sarah said, sounding worried. 'She hasn't cried that much since the day it happened.'

'Then it probably *is* the right thing. She's been bottling up her feelings.'

'I know. She's hardly spoken since it happened, has she? I keep trying to encourage her to talk about the accident, but she won't.'

'In her mind, the two things are linked. She ran into the road after Sooty . . .'

'Well, Martin, let's face it, they *are* linked! But she can't accept that it wasn't her fault.'

There was a silence for a while, apart from the sound of saucepans and things being moved around. Apparently they were preparing Sunday Lunch. That was something I knew about, from all those busy times in the pub. It made me feel a bit homesick.

'I just hope it'll cheer her up, having Oliver here,' Sarah suddenly went on. 'She's refused to go out and play with the other children all through half-term, and Grace hasn't wanted to go out without her. So they've both been stuck at home for the whole holiday. It's a good thing they're going back to school tomorrow really. It might take her mind off it.'

'Poor love, she can't really forget about the accident at all until the cast comes off her arm. And they're both obviously missing poor old Sooty.'

'Yes.' I heard Sarah's sigh, all the way from the next room. 'Brownies would have helped cheer her up – she normally loves going to Brownies.'

'But they can't hold their meetings, can they, while the hall's out of action.'

'Exactly. I don't know what's going to happen there. And it's not just Brownies, of course. The Cubs' meetings are there too and, well, everything that goes on in the village! The senior citizens' club, the WI, the nursery and the pre-school . . .'

'You're right. It's going to be a long time before the hall's fit for purpose. All those pensioners will miss their meetings, for sure. And the parents who work. How will they manage without the nursery?' He paused. 'And there was I, worrying about missing my dominoes matches in the pub.'

'Typical!' Sarah gave a little laugh. 'I don't know how everyone's going to manage, Martin. But I feel like I ought to try and do something to help. Christmas isn't that far off, and unless we can find another venue, everything's going to have to be cancelled. All the children's parties, the pensioners' dinner – everything! Perhaps I'll have a word with Brown Owl and see if she's got any ideas. That'd be a start.'

They went quiet, then, and although I was still enjoying sitting in the box, peeping over the top of it and making Grace shriek with laughter, all I really wanted to do, after hearing all that, was to sit on Rose's lap and try to cheer her up. I was sad about Sooty, too, and it made me shiver inside to think about what must have happened to him. I was beginning to realise I wasn't the only one, cat or human, with problems. My two new foster families were helping me, and I only wished I could help them in return.

When I woke up on my nice comfy armchair the next morning, I could hear Grace chatting in the kitchen and Sarah talking about breakfast and lunch boxes and something called a *PE kit*. I did my stretching and yawning, gave myself a good wash, and by the time I'd strolled into the kitchen the children had been sent upstairs to finish getting ready for school. Martin was talking quietly to Sarah, saying he hoped Rose was going to be OK at school, and that he'd see them all later.

'Aha, look who's come in for his breakfast,' he said, spotting me walking round and round the empty food dish on the floor. I gave a couple of loud meows to show how ready I was to be fed, and he laughed and bent down to stroke me. Even though I'd decided now that I liked him, I still shrank away from his touch. I couldn't help it, it was such a deep instinct in me. Then I felt bad about it, because he was feeding me and giving me a nice warm house to stay in, after all, and I hadn't meant to hurt his feelings. So I rubbed myself against his back paws a few times to make up for it.

'All right, boy! Grub's coming,' he said, getting a tin of something out of the cupboard and opening it up. Salmon! I purred my head off in gratitude and fell on the food hungrily.

Sarah was watching me. 'I'll have to stock up on tinned cat food,' she told Martin. 'We can't keep on giving him things like that.'

What a shame. But still, hopefully she'd buy nice cat food.

After Martin said goodbye and went off in the car to drive to his work, wherever that was, Sarah and the children put their coats and shoes on to walk to the school bus-stop. Grace was complaining that she was nine and a half now, and Rose was nearly eight, and they were both big enough to walk round to the bus-stop on their own, but Sarah gave her a frown and said 'Shush, Grace. I want to come with you this morning.'

Even I, with my little cat's brain, understood that it was because of Rose being upset, and having the broken paw, that she wanted to go with them. I think Grace understood too then, because she didn't say anything else. Rose hadn't said a single word since breakfast. She looked pale and sad and forgot to say goodbye to me. I wanted to go with them, but Sarah closed the door on me, calling out that she wouldn't be long. Luckily, I'd already clocked that there was a cat flap in the kitchen door because of Sooty, and it wasn't locked, so I jumped out, found my way round the side of the house and followed them down the street.

'Oh no!' Grace said when she noticed me. 'Will he get lost, Mummy?'

'I don't think so. He only lived just down the road from here before, you know. In the pub.'

Just down the road? I could hardly believe my ears. I'd been completely lost in that wood, imagining myself miles and miles from home, and yet after being carried for only a little way in Daniel's rucksack I was now *just down the road* from my pub? I felt a quiver of excitement go through me. Sure enough, as we made our way down the road I was beginning to recognise places. There was the village shop. There was the house where the noisy big black dog lived. I ran past that one quickly! And there was the village green, with the children's swings and the benches where people sat and chatted when it was warmer weather. And there . . . oh my goodness. I stopped, staring at my pub – the only proper home I'd ever known – and I felt a terrible howl of anguish rising up in my little chest. Sarah and the children had walked on, and I ran to catch them up, crying as I went.

'What's the matter with Oliver, Mummy?' Grace asked, and Sarah turned back to look from me to the blackened, ruined buildings over the road. She gazed for a minute at the sky where the pub roof used to be, the gaping empty holes where the windows were, the remains of curtains flapping in the breeze, and bits of black, burnt furniture left half in and half out of doorways. She turned and looked at the village hall next door, which looked like a giant animal had sat on it and made the top cave in, and then she shook her head, bent down to stroke me and said to the children:

'He's crying because his home's burnt down.'

'Poor Oliver,' said Grace. Then she looked up. 'Mummy,' she said in a hurried, anxious little voice. 'That boy in front of us is Michael Potts in my class, and he's not very nice.'

Sure enough, there was a young male human, a bit bigger than Grace, staring at us from further down the road.

'Has your sister got another cat?' he called out to Grace. 'Is she going to kill that one too?' And he laughed in a horrible, rude way. I don't know why he thought it was

41

funny, but it certainly wasn't. I was so furious to think that it might start Rose crying again, I didn't even stop to consider the fact that he was a strange male. I ran straight up to him, hissing and spitting with anger, my fur up on end, my ears flat to my head and my tail huge with threat. I had my claws out and would have jumped up his legs and scratched him if Sarah hadn't come running after me.

'Hey, hey, that's enough, Oliver!' she said, but she wasn't being cross with me. She sounded quite pleased in a funny way.

'That cat's dangerous,' the nasty boy said. He'd backed away from me and was looking at me with big frightened eyes. 'You ought to keep him indoors.'

'Cats go wherever they want,' Sarah said calmly. 'That's why sometimes, sadly, they get hit by cars on the road. I'm sure you heard that's what happened to our Sooty.'

She was giving him a hard stare that made him open his eyes even wider.

'Y . . , yes, I know,' he said in a scaredy-cat squeak.

'So I presume you also heard that Rose ran into the road to try to save him?' she went on. 'She did it without thinking, but she was too late. She got hurt herself. She was a very brave little girl.'

The boy just stood there, looking at the ground, shifting from paw to paw, and Sarah took hold of both the girls and said, 'Come on, children, or you'll be late for the bus,' and they walked on.

Me? I tried to give the boy the same sort of stare Sarah had used on him. All cats know that's supposed to be a hostile signal. But by now my bravery had fizzled out a bit and I don't think it worked very well.

'Stupid ginger cat!' he hissed at me as soon as Sarah was out of earshot.

Ginger-and-white, actually. I was proud of my white bits.

It was all too much for me. I watched until they'd all turned the corner, and then I went back the way we'd come. This time I couldn't even bear to look when I passed the pub.

CHAPTER
FIVE

Sarah seemed to be a long time coming back from the school bus. I went out in the garden and had a look around. There were a couple of big fat woodpigeons out there, always good for a spot of chasing, they're so slow and stupid. I amused myself with them for a while until it got boring. Then I climbed the fence at the side and looked down into the little paved area outside Nicky and Daniel's house. From here, their house looked even smaller, a bit like the toy house I'd seen in the children's bedroom, with only one window at the bottom and one at the top. The roof was slanting and covered with moss and everything about it looked sort of wonky. It reminded me of an old tatty cat, struggling to stay upright, whereas Sarah and Martin's house, although it wasn't big like the pub, was younger and smarter, like a sleek, well-fed, well-groomed cat. Much like myself. No need to laugh, little kitten. I may not be a youngster anymore but I'm still in my prime, let me tell you. I could still give a little kitten like you a run for your money.

Haven't they given you a name yet, by the way? I can't keep on calling you Little Kitten forever. What's that you say? They're calling you *Kitty*? What sort of a name is that for a boy cat, for heaven's sake? Oh, I see, it's just till they decide on a good name. Well, they'd better hurry up about it. I'm not calling you *Kitty* in front of all the other cats. You'd be a laughing stock.

Anyway, so I jumped down into Nicky and Daniel's little yard and had a sniff around, but there wasn't much there, and they had no cat flap so I couldn't get inside the house. I remembered them saying they both went out to work all day, so I thought I'd go back and see them later. It was cold, so I was glad to get back inside Sarah's nice warm kitchen and have a little nap in Sooty's old bed.

A little later, I heard voices coming from the lounge. It was Sarah, and another female, and they were making peculiar noises that made my fur stand up in alarm.

'A-cootchy-cootchy-coo!' Sarah was going. 'A-boo, cootchy-coo!'

Was she trying to imitate a pigeon? I sat up in bed, my head on one side, wondering whether it was safe to go into the lounge and look.

'Ah, look at his little face!' she was saying now. 'Do you want your dum-dum, diddums?'

Dum-dum, diddums? Was this some foreign language I hadn't come across before? One of the regulars in the pub used to speak something they called Spanish, and someone else spoke normal English but with a very funny accent they called *American*, but this was different altogether.

'He probably wants feeding again,' the other woman said in a more normal voice, sounding kind of weary. 'Is that what you want, little man? Milky-poos?'

Milky-poos? It sounded disgusting, put like that. I slunk out of the kitchen, keeping to the walls, and peered around the lounge door. There was Sarah, sitting on the sofa with the other woman, and on her lap was this tiny, tiny human.

Honestly, he was probably smaller than me! Well, I knew humans had kittens, obviously, like we do, but I never realised they started off so small. Not only that, he'd now started meowing just like a cat-kitten. It was all very confusing. As I watched, the new woman lifted him up, undid her shirt and started feeding him. This made a bit more sense. It reminded me of being fed by my own mother, along with my brothers and sisters, before . . . everything terrible happened, long ago. I couldn't help myself from giving a little mew of sorrow at the bittersweet memory, and both women looked up and saw me.

'Oh, here he is!' Sarah said. 'Oliver, our new house guest – but of course, you've met him already.'

Had she?

'Oh yes.' The other female smiled at me. She looked nice, probably a slightly younger female than Sarah, but her dark hair was tied back off her face as if she'd done it in a hurry, and her eyes looked like she needed a good long cat-nap. 'What a little hero he is!'

A hero? What could she mean? She must be muddling me up with some other good-looking ginger-and-white cat.

'I remember him from the pub,' she went on. 'We used to go there for a pie and a pint every Friday night, before we . . .' Her face went a bit funny, then, like she was trying not to cry. 'When I was working,' she went on quickly. 'Before I had the baby.'

'You'll be able to go out again, Hayley. Jack's only a couple of months old, and things will get easier. When he's stopped needing the night feeds, you'll be able to get a babysitter.'

'Will I?' she said, sounding like she didn't believe it. 'Tom booked a table for us for Christmas Eve, you know, as a special treat. He said by then the baby should have settled down a bit, and I could ask one of the mums at the mother-and-baby group to recommend a babysitter. But now the pub's gone.'

'Couldn't you go somewhere else? If you can get babysitters for an evening, Tom could drive you into town to the Italian restaurant, or that big chain pub. They do lovely cheap meals there.'

'But there's no mother-and-baby group now either! I'm so disappointed! I'd only just joined, and I was looking forward to getting to know some of the other mums with babies around here. It's not just Little Broomford mums who come to the group, apparently. They come from Great Broomford and all the other villages around here, and how else can we get to know people, stuck out here in the back of beyond?' Her voice was starting to sound like the wail of a cat crying. I wondered if I should go and rub my head against her legs. 'I miss my colleagues in the office. I miss seeing lots of people every day. I even miss commuting on the bloody train.'

'Of course you do,' Sarah soothed her. 'It's a huge change, being at home with a little baby, after being out at work every day. But you'll soon get used to it, really you will. Meanwhile, if you and Tom want to book somewhere for an evening out around Christmas time, *I* could babysit for you.'

'Oh! Sarah, I couldn't expect you to do that. You'll be busy – you've got your own children. I hope you don't think I was hinting.' She went red and put her paw over her mouth.

'Of course I don't!' Sarah smiled at her. 'I remember what it was like, when my girls were babies. You need something to look forward to.'

'Well, I *was* looking forward to Christmas this year. Jack's first Christmas – it sounded so exciting. But now, I'm just so tired all the time, I can't even be bothered to think about it. And I wish I didn't feel so lonely. Don't get me wrong, it's been really lovely talking to *you*. It was so kind of you to invite me round like this.'

'It was nice of *you* to ask me if everything was all right,' Sarah said. 'I didn't even notice you sitting there on the village green till I was on my way back from the bus-stop. You saw the whole thing?'

'I did, yes. What a brave cat Oliver was, fronting up to that Michael Potts like a right little tiger! Scared the life out of him, didn't he?'

A *little tiger*! I don't mind saying, I purred out loud with pride. Both the women were laughing and giving me affectionate smiles. I did a happy circuit of the coffee table, and then rubbed myself against Sarah's legs and gave her a blink of my eyes as a kiss. She was one of my humans now and I wanted her to know that I liked her.

When the children came back from school, I was pleased to see that Rose looked a bit happier.

'Her friends were nice to her, about Sooty,' Grace said. 'And everyone wrote on her plaster – look!'

Sarah smiled as she read some of the messages. 'That's nice,' she said. 'They've all written about how brave you were, Rose.'

'And *Oliver* was brave, too, this morning, wasn't he, Mummy!' Grace said, running over to me and giving me a cuddle. I purred again with pleasure. I'd never been called *brave* or a *tiger* before today. I'd probably never *been* brave before!

Then Rose came over to me too. She was smiling and stroking me with her good paw, and when she said in a quiet little voice, 'I love you, Oliver,' Grace and Sarah both laughed out loud like they were really pleased and excited. I felt pretty good myself, too.

After I'd had my dinner, I decided it was time to pop back next door and see if Daniel and Nicky were home. Because they didn't have a cat flap, I had to stand at the front door making as much noise as possible, and it wasn't long before Nicky let me in. She seemed really happy to see me.

'Look who's here,' she called to Daniel. 'Ah, it's lovely to see you again, Oliver. Have you had a good day?'

I wanted to tell her all about being a brave tiger, and cheering little Rose up, but I just had to make do with a lot of purring.

'I'll give him a saucer of milk. I'm sure *that* won't strain the finances too much,' she said, going to the fridge.

'I get paid this week,' Daniel said. 'Maybe then we can help Martin and Sarah out a bit with feeding him.'

Just then, the phone started ringing and he answered it while I drank my lovely milk.

'Yes, this is Daniel,' he was saying. 'Oh yes, hello, George. I know, I was here when Martin called you. Oh, well, of course not! You've had such a terrible shock, and such a lot to think about, I can understand that you wouldn't have been able to think straight. Yes, it must have been a relief to know Oliver's all right. He's here in the kitchen with me right now, actually, drinking some milk! Yes, he's absolutely fine, don't worry.' There was a long pause, and then: 'Oh, no, George – no, it's actually . . . no, look, it's not us you need to give it to. No, listen, we're not actually feeding him – Martin and Sarah are. We're kind-of sharing looking after Oliver, you see, because Nicky and I are out at work all day, and Sarah and the kids are more company for him. Yes, and I know they're happy to do it. Well, you'd need to ask them, really, but honestly, you mustn't send *us* any money – he's not costing us anything, you see. No, that's just a drop of milk! Honestly, Sarah's feeding him! OK, well you discuss it with them, then. Nice to speak to you. Hope you're settling down all right with your sister. Bye.'

'Was George offering to pay for Oliver's keep?' Nicky asked as I washed myself thoroughly after finishing the milk. She'd come to listen at the kitchen doorway.

I meowed at the sound of George's name. He must have been thinking about me, missing me, to phone them like that.

'Yes, he said he felt terrible for not suggesting it the other day. He'd been so overwhelmed with relief about

53

Oliver being OK. And now he wanted to send us a cheque! Even when I explained that we weren't the ones feeding him, he tried to argue that it must be costing us something to give him a drop of milk now and then.'

'Ah, it was nice of him to offer. And that's good if he's going to send next door a bit of money to help with the food.'

'Yes. I don't feel quite so guilty about it now. It was pretty embarrassing having to admit to Martin that we're so hard up we couldn't even buy a few cans of cat food.'

'Perhaps my parents were right, Dan.' Nicky sounded sad. 'We should have waited. Moving in together before we had enough money was stupid, wasn't it. We can barely even pay the rent.'

'But it was awful living with your parents. I'm sorry, Nick, it was good of them to let us, but we both know it wasn't working out. They don't really approve of me, and it's affected *your* relationship with them.' He sighed. 'Maybe they *were* right. Maybe you should have found someone better, someone with more money who could support you properly.'

'Don't say that! You know I didn't want anyone else.' She put her arms round him and hugged him, and I felt so sorry for them both I joined in, walking round both their legs and stroking them with my head until they started to laugh.

'At least Oliver doesn't care whether we're rich or poor,' Daniel said.

'I don't care either. We'll manage somehow, Dan. And when my parents see how we've made a go of it, they'll change their minds, I know they will. They're not unreasonable, and it's not that they don't like you. They just worry.'

Daniel nodded and gave her another hug, and went back into the living room to read the paper. Nicky stayed in the kitchen with me for a minute, watching me finishing my wash.

'The trouble is, Ollie,' she said to me in a soft little voice that wouldn't carry into the other room, 'he doesn't know that they planned to come and see us at Christmas. They were going to stay overnight at the pub. It would've been the first time they'd made the effort to visit since we moved in. My two brothers were coming too. We can't possibly put them up here – we've only got one bedroom and it's tiny. They're not going to be impressed when I tell them they can't come.'

Oh dear. I didn't really understand why her parents seemed to have made Nicky and Daniel unhappy. But it was pretty obvious that they weren't going to be able to stay at the pub now. I was beginning to see that the fire was making a lot of difficulties for my new human friends, as well as for me and George. If only I could think of a way to help.

CHAPTER
SIX

The next day when the children came home from school again, they had two other little girls with them.

'Show us, then!' one of them was saying to Grace as they walked in the door. 'What sort of cat is he? Is he friendly?'

I was in my favourite chair in the lounge, having a little doze. I opened one eye and watched them standing in the doorway.

'Yes, when he gets to know you,' Grace replied. 'But he's a bit shy at first, so don't crowd him, please.' She sounded very proud and important to be showing me off. 'Let Rose pick him up. He likes her best.'

I thought that was nice of her, and I could tell Rose did too, because she was smiling as she came over to me.

'Hello, Oliver,' she whispered. 'We've brought some friends to meet you. Don't be frightened, they're very nice.'

It was probably the most I'd heard her speak. I let her pick me up, and she carried me to the sofa where she sat with me on her lap and beckoned the other girls to join us.

'He's lovely!' squealed one of them. 'Can we stroke him?'

'Yes, but very gently,' Grace said. 'He's still getting used to us. Daddy says he was always shy with strangers, when he lived in the pub, and didn't like people touching him.'

The two friends put their little paws gently on my head and back and stroked me very carefully. It was nice. I didn't mind them. Human kittens generally seemed kind, apart from that nasty big male the previous morning.

'He's purring,' one of them said, excitedly. 'He likes us!'

'He's not a bit like your other cat,' the second girl said – and then she put her paw over her mouth and added, 'Oh! Sorry, Rose. I didn't say it to upset you.'

'It's all right,' Rose said quietly.

'It's just that he's different, isn't he. Sooty was so big and black and, well, quite old, but Oliver's a really pretty colour and he looks like he's not much more than a kitten.'

What a nice child. I stretched my neck towards her appreciatively. She was obviously a connoisseur of cats.

'I know.' Rose gave a little smile. 'I'm glad he's different. I wouldn't have liked it if he was like Sooty. It would have made me cry to look at him.'

I couldn't get over how much Rose was talking. Sarah had come into the room behind the children and was listening to them, smiling.

'Would you all like a glass of milk and some biscuits, girls?' she said, and they scrambled off to the kitchen.

'Can we play with Oliver afterwards?'

'Can we give him some milk?'

'Have you got any toys for him?'

They were chatting away excitedly, looking back at me as they went.

'Is he yours forever now?' I heard one of them say after they'd gone out of sight.

'No.' Grace sounded disappointed. 'Mummy says we're sharing him with next door, but only till his owner comes back from London. But it might be quite a long time.'

'Maybe your mum and dad will get you another cat the same as him, after he goes.'

And it was Rose's little voice that answered: 'I hope so. I want one *exactly* like Oliver.'

Later on, after we'd all tired ourselves out with a game of jumping out at each other from behind the sofa, and another one of rolling a ball of wool across the floor and pouncing after it, the friends got their coats on and waited for their parents to come and walk them home. It was dark outside, and raining, and I was wondering how much longer I could put off going out to empty my bladder. I've always been a very clean cat and it would have been unthinkable to me to have an accident indoors, especially when I was really a guest in the house. But the sound of the wind and rain was putting me off. I sat with my nose against the cat flap, thinking about it, and the children watched me, laughing.

'We could study Oliver for our Brownies' "Friend to Animals" badge,' one of them said suddenly.

'Oh, yes, that's a good idea,' Grace said. 'All of us in our Six could work on the badge together!' She sounded very excited. 'As I'm Sixer of the Foxes, I think I should be the one to tell Brown Owl we want to do it.'

Foxes? I turned round and stared at them in horror. What was all this about foxes?

'But we aren't having any Brownie meetings, are we,' the other friend said, sadly, 'because of the village hall.'

'So?' Grace said. 'I'll ask Mummy if all the Foxes can come and meet *here* every week.'

I'd heard enough. I pushed the cat flap open and jumped out into the garden. It might have been cold and wet, but if they were going to start having foxes in the house, I was going to have to get used to making myself scarce.

I admit I was a coward where foxes were concerned. And yes, it was true, I'd always been a bit of a scaredy-cat about being touched by strange humans. But ever since the incident with the young male who was horrible to Rose, and especially after I'd been called a brave boy, and a tiger, because of it, I could actually feel myself becoming bolder and more adventurous. I did sometimes have bad dreams about the night the pub caught fire, and getting lost in the woods. And when the other nightmare – the one I'd been having since I was a little kitten – happened, I woke up shaking all over with my heart racing, just as I'd always done. But I was beginning to realise that most humans seemed to be all right, after all – that although George would always be my favourite, he wasn't the only one who could be kind and gentle.

When I lived in the pub, I only ventured out into the village when George had to go out and I was bored of being on my own. There were a few other cats nearby and we sometimes met round the back of the shop, where the dustbins were. So a day or two later, when Sarah was out and I was alone in their house, I decided I'd recovered enough from the shock of the fire to risk a little walk around the village on my own.

I went straight to the shop and looked round the back, but just my luck, none of my cat friends were playing there that morning. I'd been looking forward to telling them all about my heroic rescue of George, to say nothing of the way I'd escaped the fox *and* seen off the aggressive young human. Me, a scaredy-cat? They'd soon change their opinion of me! But it seemed like I'd have to save my stories for another day.

I wandered back round to the street, and there in front of the shop were two human females, both pushing those wheeled contraptions they called prams, and trying to chat to each other over the mewing and meowing noises coming from inside them.

'Oh look,' said one of the women. 'It's Oliver, George's cat from the pub. We were wondering what had happened to him. I hope he hasn't just been living rough somewhere since the fire.'

'He doesn't *look* like he's been living rough,' the other one said.

'No. Hopefully someone's taken him in. Is someone looking after you, Oliver?'

'Yes,' I meowed. 'I've got two nice foster homes, thank you.' But of course, neither of them spoke Cat, so they just kept looking at me as they carried on their conversation together about how sad it was having no mother-and-baby group meetings.

I wandered off, further down the street to the village green in case my friend Tabby and the other cats were hanging out there instead. But instead of them, I found another human with a pram. It was Hayley, who'd been at Sarah's house with the baby Jack, on the day of my heroic confrontation with Michael Potts. She was sitting on the bench, holding the handle of her pram, and just staring at the ground. She looked up when I trotted towards her, and said: 'Oh, hello, Oliver.' But she didn't sound particularly happy.

I jumped up onto the other end of the bench and meowed a hello to her, but she just sighed and said, 'Are you all on your own today too?'

I thought it was a strange thing to say, because obviously she *wasn't* on her own – she had Jack with her. But apparently she just wanted to talk to me, even though I was only a cat, because she went on, 'I wish I could still see the friends I had at work. I shouldn't have given up my job, Oliver, but I couldn't imagine how I'd manage, commuting and working and looking after a baby, or paying a child minder. Oh, I had no idea it was all going to be so hard. I feel so tired all the time, and I suppose I'm just *lonely*. I wish I had some friends in the village. Just some other mums I could talk to about things – it would make such a difference, but now there's no mother-and-baby group.'

My ears pricked up at this. How strange, it was exactly what the other two females had been complaining about. I jumped down off the bench and meowed loudly at

Hayley, walking backwards and forwards and twitching my tail urgently at her. If we went back now, we might be in time.

'What is it, Ollie?' she said, watching me curiously but not moving an inch.

Oh, come on! I meowed impatiently, and finally she seemed to get the message.

'You want me to come with you? Back to Sarah's house perhaps? What a clever boy you are – you must have understood every word I was saying. It'd be lovely to see Sarah again, but I can't keep depending on her. She's got her own worries, and her children are older. I need . . .'

I was ignoring her now, running ahead of her down the street without even waiting for her to keep up with me. Yes! As I rounded the corner, I could see the other two women still standing outside the shop with their prams, still talking away like yappy dogs. I walked round them three times one way, and twice the other way, making them laugh and wonder aloud what I was playing at. And finally, Hayley came into view pushing her own pram, and the three women looked at each other and started to laugh as if they were already old friends.

'Anyone would think Oliver brought me here deliberately to meet you,' I heard Hayley exclaiming after they'd introduced themselves and done a bit of *Goo-goo*-ing over each other's prams. 'Silly, I know – he's not *that* clever.'

Well, honestly. Sometimes we cats don't get any credit for our intelligence. I left them to it, and went back to Sarah and Martin's house, feeling worn out and ready for a nap. It had turned out to be a busy day of helping people, but there was only so much I could do, after all. I figured that if eight- and nine-year-old girls could come up with the idea of holding their meetings in each other's homes, hopefully three fully grown females could work it out for themselves too.

CHAPTER
SEVEN

CHAPTER
SEVEN

The following day, Sarah came home from a shopping trip accompanied by yet another female. They were chatting as they went into the kitchen and started making coffee, and it sounded like, once again, it was the closing of the pub and the village hall they were worrying about.

'Anyway, Anne,' Sarah said as they came into the lounge, where I was enjoying a sunny spot on the windowsill watching the birds, 'I'm glad I bumped into you this morning. I wanted to talk to you about Brownies.'

'Yes, you see, that's another thing,' the other woman said. She looked slightly older than Sarah, with a cheerful-looking round face and a booming voice. 'I've tried *everywhere* to find a temporary venue for the meetings, but I've had no luck whatsoever. The school hall at Great Broomford is booked solidly every evening of the week for adult education classes, the folk dancing club and God knows what else. The community centre there is just the same, in fact they have a waiting list. And St Luke's church hall *did* have a couple of slots free before the fire, but it seems the Scouts and the youth club have got in ahead of us.'

'Oh. Well, at least *they're* sorted, I suppose. And it's probably easier for their age groups to get there, even if their parents don't drive. A lot of them have bikes.'

'That's true. But, sadly, I'm sending a letter to all the Brownies' parents, Sarah, explaining that unless anyone has any ideas for a venue, pack meetings are suspended indefinitely. It's such a shame. Some of the girls will have grown out of Brownies by the time we can reopen.'

'I have got one *tiny* little idea, though,' Sarah said. 'It's come about because of Oliver, actually.'

They'd both been ignoring me completely up till now, but when Sarah pointed to me, Anne gave a little chuckle of surprise.

'The pub cat? I didn't realise he was staying with you.'

And Sarah had to explain all about my escape from the fire, and rescue from the tree, and then she described how the children and their friends wanted to study me for their Brownie badge and were going to meet at the house every week. I kept my ears pricked for any mention of foxes being invited.

'That's a nice idea,' Anne said.

'Well, at least it means their Six will still be having regular meetings. I can look up what they have to do for their badge, and give them some help, and when they're ready perhaps you could come round and test them?'

'Of course I will. In fact, as Brown Owl, I think I should pop round every couple of weeks to see how they're getting on. It'll be good to keep in touch with the Foxes, even if I don't see the other children.'

There it was. Foxes *were* coming! I gave a little mew of anxiety but neither of the women seemed to notice.

'Well, this is what I was wondering, Anne,' Sarah said excitedly. 'I can't offer to hold meetings for the rest of the pack here, obviously – we wouldn't have the room. But if the Foxes meet here, couldn't the parents of some of the other girls host their own Six meetings? It would be better than nothing, and it would give them all some continuity.'

'That's a *splendid* idea.' Anne was on her feet now, looking like she wanted to jump up and down with excitement. 'I'm sure Jessica's mum would be happy to host the Badgers, and I'll talk to Molly's parents about having the Squirrels at their house. Leave it with me. Brilliant idea, Sarah. Have you ever thought about becoming a Brownie leader?'

Sarah was laughing. 'Well, maybe I should consider it. But it was all thanks to Oliver, really.'

I couldn't help feeling a surge of pleasure at this, although part of my brain was still struggling with the issue of the foxes. If badgers and squirrels were meeting at other humans' houses, and owls seemed to be involved too, why did we have to be the ones getting *foxes* here, of all things? None of these were the type of animals who should be trusted indoors, but if there was any sign of a fox here, the children could study *him* for their badges. I'd be hiding next door.

I decided to make it my routine to pop into the little house next door to see Nicky and Daniel most evenings. They seemed pleased to see me, but I felt sad that there was nothing I could do to help them with their worries. If they weren't talking about how little money they had to last the month, they were worrying about Christmas. Nicky must have told Daniel now about her parents' planned visit.

'We'll just have to explain to them about the pub,' Daniel was saying when I visited that night. 'Can't they stay at the hotel in Great Broomford instead? Or one of the pubs there?'

'They're all fully booked for Christmas week already, even though it's only the beginning of November. I've phoned around all of them. I suppose I'm just going to have to put them off, Dan, but it's going to make things even worse between us. I don't suppose they'll understand – they never do.'

'Well, to be honest, it'll save us all the worry of buying a big turkey and presents for everyone.'

'That's not exactly how we should be thinking, is it?' Nicky said, and I was surprised by how snappy she sounded. 'It was going to be our first opportunity to try and show them they were wrong, about us getting together.'

'Yes, well, we can't very well invite them round here for a Christmas lunch of beans on toast, and presents from Poundland, and let them all sleep on the living room floor, can we? Face it, Nicky, you're wasting your time trying to convince them we did the right thing. Having them stay at the pub wasn't going to help. They'd still be able to see the state we're in. We can't even afford to put the heating on. I don't know why you agreed to it in the first place.'

Nicky was sniffing and wiping her eyes. I jumped onto her lap to console her, and her tears dripped onto my head.

'Sorry, baby,' Daniel said after a few minutes. 'I didn't mean it. I just feel so frustrated about everything. I know it's my fault. I need to get a better job.'

'Well, maybe I should think about getting a *second* job, doing some waitressing or something in the evenings. If it wasn't for the fire at the pub, I could have asked there. But I can try in Great Broomford.'

'No. It should be *me* doing an extra job, if either of us do. I'll just have to look harder. Something will turn up,' Daniel said. But he didn't sound convinced. He just sounded tired, and fed up.

Most of the people I met on my walks around the village seemed to know, by now, that I was staying with my two foster families since the fire. I recognised a lot of the regulars from the pub, and several of them would say hello to me and try to stroke me.

'Same old Oliver,' one of the domino men laughed with his friend, when I scampered away as soon as he bent down to pet me. 'Friendly little cat, but timid as a mouse.'

Timid? A *mouse*? I quivered with indignation. I'd have him know that in some quarters I was known as a tiger! Feeling annoyed, I wandered a little further down one of the quiet side lanes, and sat on the wall of a little cottage similar to Daniel and Nicky's, watching some starlings squabbling over a few bits of bread someone had dropped in the front garden. One of them had his back to me and I thought what good fun it would be to creep up on him from behind and pounce. Perhaps if I caught one, I could take it home to Sarah as a thank you for looking after me. I climbed stealthily down from the wall, and lay flat in its shadow with my head down and my rear end twitching in the time-honoured way, waiting for my moment. And just as none of the stupid birds were watching and I was about to go for it, the front door of the cottage was flung open, the whole flock of starlings flew, startled, up into the trees, and a very ancient-looking human female appeared on the doorstep, waving a wooden spoon and shouting at me.

'Shoo! Go on, shoo, you horrible cat, leave the poor birds alone. I put that bread out for them. They'd starve in the winter if it wasn't for me. Go on, get lost, you scabby old stray. I don't want your smelly cat pee in my garden.'

Well! I'd never been so insulted in any of my nine lives. Scabby old *stray*? I actually had to look around to see if she was talking to someone else. I could only assume the poor ancient creature had problems with her eyesight. How else could anyone mistake a fine, sleek, well-groomed and beautifully mannered cat such as myself, in peak condition and in the prime of my life, with a *scabby old stray*? It was so ridiculous it was laughable. I decided I should probably feel sorry for her, so rather than take offence and stalk off, I stayed where I was. Pretending I hadn't even heard her nonsensical outburst, I occupied myself with having a good wash of my face to show the stupid starlings, chattering in the trees above me, that I hadn't been the least bit bothered about catching any of them in the first place. I wasn't worried about the woman, even when she started yelling again. After all, she looked far too old to come after me, let alone do me any damage.

Little kitten, I will never again make the mistake of underestimating an elderly human. I have no idea how she moved so fast. One minute she was on her doorstep, and the next, she was towering over me, her wooden spoon raised, threatening to knock me for six. All I could do was cower against the wall, spitting at her – she was blocking all my escape routes. Had I really survived the fire, and the fox, to say nothing of the terrible thing that happened when I was only a tiny kitten, just to end up being beaten to a pulp by an old woman with a spoon? I yowled out loud for help. Where were all my cat friends when I needed them?

And then, just as I thought I was done for, she stopped shouting and said: 'Just a minute. What's that? A collar?'

'Yes, a collar, you silly old woman,' I meowed at her furiously in Cat. 'I'm a proper, decent, clean-living pet, not a stray.'

Not that I'm prejudiced against strays, you understand. Most of them have fallen on hard times and deserve a bit of help. I was all too aware that I might have ended up in the same position myself, more than once now.

'Let me have a look at that,' she said, and before I could try to make a run for it, she'd grabbed hold of me in a most undignified way and held me aloft, ignoring my squawks of protest, while she peered at the writing on my identity disc. 'Oliver, eh?' she said. 'Well, Oliver, I don't know where you come from, but you can bugger off there now, and don't come back. I don't put bread out for the birds just for greedy spoilt moggies like you to come sniffing around.'

So first I was a scabby stray, and now I was a greedy spoilt moggy? I was almost too angry at the insults to be frightened of the rough way she was handling me. Just as I was trying to turn my head far enough to give her a nip with my teeth, so that she'd put me down, there was a shout from a house across the road.

'Hey, Barbara! What are you doing with the pub cat?'

Another ancient human – a male version this time. Things were going from bad to worse. But at least this one recognised me.

'Bugger off and mind your own business, Stan Middleton! I caught this damned moggy going after the birds in my garden. Or after the bread more likely, the greedy thing.'

As if I wanted her horrible stale bread, when I had Tesco value meaty chunks with tuna available to me back at my foster home.

'Put him down, woman, before you hurt the poor little sod. He's Oliver, George's cat from the Forester's Arms. He wouldn't hurt a fly. He's probably just lonely.'

'Huh,' the woman called Barbara said. 'Lonely? He doesn't know the meaning of the word. And nor do you, Stan, before you say anything. Off down the pub with your old cronies every lunchtime – I've seen you.'

'Don't talk stupid, woman. The pub's burnt down now. I'm stuck at home all day every day just the same as you. If the hall hadn't had to close as well, I might have even been reduced to joining that flipping pensioners' club of yours, sitting there with you and all the other old women, nattering about your knitting and your TV soaps.'

'TV soaps?' she shrieked – and I finally managed to wriggle out of her arms and shoot off out of her reach. 'I can't even watch the damned soaps any more. My telly's broken and my son-in-law's too busy to come round and fix it, the selfish little bugger. I've a good mind to send back his Christmas present to the mail order people. I haven't finished paying for it yet.'

'Same as my selfish granddaughter – no time for us old people, that's their trouble,' I heard Stan saying as I slunk away. Neither of them seemed to be taking any notice of me anymore. 'If you weren't such a stubborn old woman I'd offer to come and look at your TV for you, but I don't suppose you'll let me inside your house. Still sulking about that shrub I trimmed for you, I suppose. Thought I was doing you a favour, but you can't please some people.'

When I was at a safe distance I turned back to watch them. Stan, the old male, had crossed the road now and they were talking together by Barbara's gate.

'Fix TVs, can you? I don't suppose you're any good,' she was saying. 'Still, you'd better come in and have a try, otherwise I'll never hear the end of it. I suppose you'll be wanting a slice of my fruit cake in return. You needn't think you'll get it on one of my best plates. And take your shoes off before you walk on the carpet – I don't know where you've been!'

I was feeling quite sorry for Stan. But, you know what? Even from that distance, I could see he was grinning all over his face as he followed her into her cottage. Sometimes, little kitten, even an experienced cat like myself can't make head nor tail of human behaviour. I trotted home to Sarah's house as fast as I could, spent a good long time licking my sore paws where the woman had held me in her grip, and then had a well-deserved sleep to get over the experience.

CHAPTER
EIGHT

CHAPTER
EIGHT

The next day was a Saturday. You'll learn to tell the difference with these human-invented days, little kitten, when you're a grown-up cat like me. Saturdays and Sundays are when the children don't go to school and most of the adults don't go to work, not to be confused with holidays and special days like Christmas and Easter. Yes, I know it's very muddling but humans don't seem to be able to manage like we do, with every day being whatever we want it to be. Anyway, on this particular Saturday, I was sitting on Sarah's windowsill when I saw something coming along the road that made me sit up straight and meow with excitement. At first I thought I might be seeing things, but as it came closer and finally stopped outside the house, I knew I was right. It was the same big old blue car I'd known for nearly my whole life, and there, getting out of it, was my very own human, George.

I jumped down from the windowsill and rushed for the front door, walking round and round in frantic circles and meowing my head off. Sarah came out of the kitchen wiping her hands on a tea-towel, and the children came tumbling downstairs from playing in their bedroom.

'What on earth's all the fuss about, Ollie?' Sarah said, as the children stood there giggling at my excitement. 'Do you want to go out? What's wrong with using the cat flap?'

81

And then the doorbell rang, and I almost climbed up the door, I was so beside myself.

'Who can that be?' Sarah said as she went to open it. And then: 'Oh! Hello!'

I feel a little embarrassed now, telling you this, but the fact is, I went slightly loopy. I was so overcome with joy when George bent down to stroke me, I leapt straight into his arms, nearly knocking him over. I was climbing all round his neck, licking his face, purring fit to bust. I just couldn't contain myself. Everyone was laughing, George included.

'What a welcome,' he said. 'Whoa, calm down, boy, you'll have me over.'

By now, Martin, who'd been outside in the shed doing what he described as his *Saturday pottering* (I have no idea what it was, and I suspected Sarah didn't either), had heard the commotion and come back indoors.

'George!' he said, trying to shake his hand, but having difficulty because I was clinging to him like a limpet. 'Great to see you, mate. Are you back in the village?'

'No, sadly not. Just visiting.'

'Well, Ollie's pleased to see you, at any rate. Stay and have some lunch with us if you've got time.'

'Thanks, I will, if you're sure.'

So we all went through to the kitchen, and George sat at the table with me on his lap, snuggling up to him and purring contentedly.

'So how has he been?' George asked, nodding down at me.

'Brilliant,' Sarah said at once. 'We've loved having him here, haven't we, children?'

'Yes,' they both chorused, and Rose added quietly, 'I want to keep him forever.'

'No, remember what I told you?' Martin said gently. 'Oliver is George's cat, and he's only staying with us until George can come back and look after him again.'

'But that won't be for quite a long time. And I'm sure he'll still come and visit you, and play with you, when he's back with me,' George added.

'Of course I will,' I meowed, but needless to say, nobody understood me. Sometimes it's very frustrating that humans don't learn Cat. They think they're so much cleverer than us, it wouldn't hurt them to try.

Well, they sat around the table drinking tea and eating toasted sandwiches, and Sarah finally lured me off George's lap by putting some bits of cheese down for me. Then afterwards the children went off to play but I stayed with the adults, wanting to enjoy every minute of George's company before he went away again.

'I'm so grateful to you for taking care of Oliver for me,' he was saying to Sarah and Martin. 'I couldn't possibly have had him with me at my sister's place, and besides, it's better for him to be here in the village where he knows his way around.'

'Of course it is. And he's been no trouble at all,' Sarah said. 'But he's not with us all the time. He goes next door to Nicky and Daniel a lot, too.'

'So: tell me who I should make this cheque out to,' George said, pulling his wallet out of his pocket. 'I was going to post it, but I really wasn't sure about the arrangements. Daniel told me on the phone the other day that you were buying all the cat food.'

'Well, it's probably fifty-fifty,' Martin said, giving Sarah a quick glance. 'Don't worry about us, but I daresay he's eating Nicky and Daniel out of house and home – you know what cats are like.'

I was a bit puzzled by this, as I knew perfectly well what the arrangement was, and so did Martin. He'd agreed that he and Sarah would be the ones feeding me. Although Nicky did occasionally give me a saucer of milk or a few scraps, I had a feeling Martin was just trying to be kind to them.

'OK, look, I'll make the cheque out to you, Martin, if you don't mind, and leave you to divvy it up between you. And . . . jump down a minute, will you, Ollie? I've got a few things in the car to bring in.'

'This is far too much,' Martin was protesting, looking at the cheque.

'No it's not. It's for the month, all right? I'll try to get down here roughly once a month to settle up with you, or if it's easier, I could just buy a month's supply of food and bring it with me.'

'No, look, there's no need . . .'

'But I thought a cheque might be better, so that if I can't get down here, I can just post it.'

'But, listen, George, I don't want to be personal, but are you all right for money? I mean, with the pub being out of action?'

'Oh yes, I'm fine, mate – don't worry about me. The brewery's looking after me. I'm only a tenant landlord, you know. Straight after the fire, when I told them I'd got to move to London for the duration of the rebuilding work, they found me a temporary job in a local pub close by, that's just reopened after refurbishment. I'm doing shifts there at the moment, but luckily everywhere is busy, with Christmas coming up, so I should have full-time work soon. They've got the chef from the Forester's a job too, in Great Broomford. I couldn't do anything for the barmaids, unfortunately – they were just employed on a casual basis. But I've heard on the grapevine that they've both managed to get some work here and there in town.'

'So, in some ways,' Sarah said, 'it's fortunate that it's the busy season.'

'Yes.' He frowned and sighed. 'But not for the people here who had bookings for meals and parties in the Forester's, and even rooms booked for family over Christmas.'

'I know.' Sarah looked sad too. 'But it's not your fault, George, and everyone will just have to make other arrangements, if they can. It's not the end of the world, and the most important thing is that you weren't hurt in the fire.'

'Thanks to Ollie,' George said, giving me another stroke now even though he'd made me get off his lap. 'If he hadn't woken me up, that night, I hate to think what would've happened.'

Everyone went quiet then, even me, not wanting to think about it. They'd been talking earlier about what might have started the fire, and apparently the 'investigators' – whoever they were – believed it was an electrical fault, something to do with some wiring. I didn't know what that meant, but I was glad nobody thought it was George's fault. Or mine.

George went out to the car, then, and came back carrying two big bags.

'Just a little token of my thanks,' he said, putting them on the table.

'But you've given us the money, George,' Sarah said, staring open-mouthed at the bags.

'These are just some things for Ollie, and some little bits for the kids – so you can't say no,' he said with a smile. 'Now, it's been great seeing you, and thanks for the lunch, but I'm going to have to get back as I'm working tonight.'

'Good to see you too, mate,' Martin said, shaking his hand. 'Thanks for the cheque – and for all this, but you didn't have to.'

'I miss my boy,' George said by way of a reply. He picked me up and gave me another quick cuddle, and I purred into his ear, wishing frantically that he didn't have to go. 'I'll see you again soon, Ollie. Be good. It'll probably be nearly Christmas before I can get back again,' he added to Sarah and Martin as he walked to the door.

I meowed to myself sadly for ages after he'd gone. But when Sarah started unpacking the bags, she found so many exciting things for me, I almost forgot to be upset. There was a new blanket – soft and fluffy with a pattern of paw prints all over it – a toy mouse stuffed with catnip, just the right size for throwing in the air and catching with my claws, some sparkly little balls to play with, a bag of my favourite cat-treats and, best of all, a little hammock made of furry material that hooked over a radiator, for me to lie in. Sarah was laughing as she watched Martin fix it over the radiator in the lounge.

'Look at that, Ollie,' she said. 'What a lovely warm, cosy bed for you, for the winter.'

I jumped straight into it, turned around a couple of times (although there wasn't much room and I nearly fell out on the first attempt), did a bit of scraping at the furry surface the way we cats like to, and finally snuggled down, purring myself to sleep as I thought fondly of George choosing my presents. I was beginning to realise what a lucky little cat I was, after all.

When I woke up, there was another surprise. It was dark, the curtains had been drawn, the children must have gone to bed – and sitting on the sofa holding glasses of drink, like the ones people had in the pub, were Nicky and Daniel from next door. Normally I'd have had my dinner by now, and then gone in to see them, but I must have had a much deeper and longer nap than usual, in my new hammock.

'It's really nice of you both to ask us round,' Nicky was saying.

'Well,' Sarah said, 'we just thought that if you weren't doing anything tonight, it'd make a change to get together for a chat. Would you like some crisps?' She passed them a little bowl, and watching them crunching away, I realised how hungry I was. I jumped out of my hammock, yawning and stretching my legs.

'Oh, look who's finally woken up,' Martin laughed. 'I suppose you want some dinner, Ollie.'

Of course I did! I followed him out to the kitchen, purring with anticipation, and did a few circuits of the place where they normally put my dish, while I waited for him to open the tin. When I'd finally finished eating, been outside for a call of nature and then had a good wash, there seemed to be a serious conversation going on, back in the lounge.

'We absolutely can't accept it,' Nicky was saying, looking a bit pink in the face. 'We haven't been feeding Ollie at all – only a spot of milk occasionally. It's your money.'

'Seriously, guys,' Martin said, 'George wanted you to have it. He wanted to show his appreciation to *all* of us for taking care of Ollie – making him comfortable and stopping him from being lonely. It's not just about the food.'

'Oh.' Nicky gave Daniel an anxious look. 'Well, I don't know what to say. I mean, it's very nice of him, but we love having Ollie popping in for visits anyway.'

'If we accept the money,' Daniel said firmly, 'we'll take over feeding him his evening meals. It's not fair, otherwise.'

Martin shrugged. 'Shall we just say that whoever's house he's in at the time can feed him?'

I pricked up my ears. If I was a crafty cat, I could do well out of this. I could have dinner in one house, and then nip next door and get a second helping. But then I remembered how worried Daniel and Nicky were about money. No, that wouldn't be right. Maybe I'd let them feed me occasionally, so they didn't feel unhappy about George's money, but I wasn't going to take advantage, tempting though it was.

'OK, we'll stock up on cat food with the money,' Nicky said.

'Only a few tins,' Sarah suggested with a smile. 'We don't want Ollie getting greedy and cadging extra meals, do we?'

They all laughed then, and I felt so embarrassed I had to turn away and pretend to wash my face again. How had they guessed what I'd been thinking?

'George has been far too generous with his cheque,' Martin said. 'We won't need all our share either, to say nothing of the presents.'

'Oh yes, I noticed the new bed on the radiator,' Nicky said.

'He loves it already. It must be so warm and cosy for him. But there were presents for the children, too – books, and games, and jigsaws – they thought Christmas had come early! So you see, we've had more than our fair share of George's gratitude.' She smiled at Nicky and added quietly, 'Please don't feel bad about accepting your share.'

That settled, the talk turned to Christmas.

'To be honest,' Nicky said, taking tiny sips of her drink, and finally putting the glass down as if she'd decided she didn't like it, 'I'm not looking forward to it.'

'Oh, why not?' Sarah asked.

Next thing I knew, the whole story was pouring out, about Nicky's parents, and the arguments, and the Christmas visit that was supposed to be their opportunity to make up with them, until the fire in the pub put paid to their stay.

'We're going to have to cancel them,' Daniel explained. 'We haven't got any room to put them up. Nicky's two younger brothers would be coming too, as they're only twelve and fourteen.'

I saw Sarah and Martin giving each other a look.

'Well, there must be a way round it,' Sarah said. 'Let us have a think.'

'I can't see *any* way, other than cancelling the visit. There's nowhere else in the village they can stay, and everywhere in Great Broomford and the other villages is fully booked.' Nicky shrugged. 'Dan says it's pointless having them come for Christmas anyway while we can't afford any luxuries.'

'It's going to be a disappointing Christmas for a lot of people here,' Martin said. 'Nowhere to hold the pensioners' party or the children's parties. No Christmas nights out at the pub . . .'

'Not even for poor Ollie,' Sarah said, smiling at me. They all laughed then, and I was glad really, because the conversation had been getting a bit sad.

'Actually it might not have been all fun and games for Ollie at the pub at Christmas time,' Martin said. 'It always got so busy, with a lot of people coming into the pub who didn't know him, and didn't realise he didn't like being stroked or petted by strangers – especially strange men.'

'He seems to have got used to both of *us* now, though, doesn't he,' Daniel said.

'Yes. We should be honoured.'

'Do you know if there's any reason for it? I mean, sometimes animals are scared of strangers if they've been ill-treated or something like that.' Daniel was holding his hand out towards me as he spoke, and I walked towards him, purring, and let him stroke my head, to show him I trusted him now. 'Has George had him ever since he was a kitten?'

'Yes.' Martin nodded. 'But you're right, he came with a history. George told me about it once. It's very sad.'

When I realised he was going to tell the others about my horrible start in life, I decided it was time to go to bed. I didn't want to hear it. It was bad enough having lived through it.

CHAPTER
NINE

All right, little kitten – do I really have to call you Kitty? – yes, I suppose it's about time I told you what happened to me. You have to understand, I don't find it easy to talk about. But perhaps it'll be good for you to realise that not all little kittens have a nice start in life, like you have, with a kind family and plenty to eat right from the start, to say nothing of having a wise older friend like me to look after you and teach you the ways of the world.

So, where do I start? With my earliest memories, I suppose. I vaguely remember being nursed by my mother, but it's only a dim, distant recollection of warmth and softness and lovely milkiness, lost to me so soon after I was born. I was one of five kittens, and my brothers and sisters were the first things I saw when my eyes started to open. My eyesight wasn't very good at first – yours will have been the same – but I was aware of the others as we all clambered over each other, competing for our mother's milk. Our little ears didn't work at first either, but gradually I became aware of the sound of my mother purring as she groomed us, and the funny little squeaks my siblings made. Obviously we were too young to have any idea where we were, but it was dry and warm, and our bed was on some kind of rough material. There was nobody else in my little world at that time – just my mother, my two sisters and two brothers.

Then everything went badly wrong. One day, soon after my ears and eyes had started to work properly, we were all startled by a sudden loud noise, and a gust of cold fresh air. My mother jumped up, trying to hide us all under her body as we kittens scrambled around on the bed in fright. We were only just beginning to learn to walk and, I have to say, I was the best at it. I'd managed to stray off the bedding once or twice, but my legs were wobbly and I couldn't wait to get back to my mother's warmth. Now, though, I was cowering under her tummy, shaking with fear.

'What the hell?' someone shouted, and there were heavy footsteps coming towards us. 'Bloody cat – how did you get in here? Bloody shed's been locked up for weeks. Drat, should have fixed that damned window, might have known all the pesky strays in the neighbourhood would get in. Get out of it – go on, clear off, you manky old thing.'

He was looming over us now. I could feel my siblings shaking as hard as I was. My mother was hissing and spitting, her whole body taut, her tail suddenly twice its normal size. You have to remember I'd never seen a human before, and I had no idea what they were. But this one was big, loud, and very angry, and my mother was making him even angrier.

'Get off me, you vicious brute,' he shouted at her as she dug her claws and her teeth into his huge hairy front paws. 'Ouch! Right, that's it – I'm gonna get you in this sack and . . .' There was a pause. His horrible red face and bulging eyes had come suddenly into focus. 'Blimey,' he exclaimed. 'Bloody kittens too.'

By now we were all squeaking and mewing in distress. Our mother was trying frantically to hide us, but he made a grab for us, one at a time, by our tails, our necks, whatever he could get hold of as we tried desperately to crawl out of his reach.

'You horrible little vermin can go in the sack first,' he said, and he pulled our bedding out from under us all, shook it so that it opened into a kind of big bag, and started dropping us in it, one by one. All the time our mother was shrieking at him and attacking him with her claws, until he threw her onto the floor and held her down with one of his huge great back paws. I was the last kitten to be dropped into the sack, and as he grabbed me by the neck I was just in time to see him kick my poor mother so hard, she wailed in pain and shot of the shed door. I can't tell you how hard I cried as I fell down into the darkness of that sack and joined my siblings in a heap at the bottom.

'Come back 'ere, you,' the human was shouting after my mother. I heard him run out of the shed, still shouting, but he was soon back, muttering about catching her next time he saw her. 'Meanwhile, let's get rid of this bag of vermin,' he said, and the next thing we knew, we were being lifted up in the air and swung along, falling over each other and squeaking with fear.

I can see I've upset you already, little kitten, and you haven't heard it all yet. Are you sure you want me to go on? I did warn you it wasn't a nice story. You're not going to have nightmares, are you? Look, I can promise you there's a happy ending. If there wasn't, I wouldn't be here with you now, curled up nice and cosy on this cushion together with the sunshine coming through the window, would I? But yes, you're quite right, that was the last time I ever saw my mother. Well, we all have to leave our mothers, as you know, but I was still too young, and of course, the circumstances weren't exactly ideal. But since I've grown up, I've always told myself I'm glad she got away from that horrible man. I know she wouldn't have left us if she'd had any choice in the matter.

Well, there we all were in that dark sack and, of course, I don't actually know how long we were in it, or where we were taken, but when we felt ourselves being dumped on the ground, we all started crying as loudly as we could – which wasn't very loud – to be let out. For a long, long time we heard nothing outside the sack apart from birds singing. We were all hungry, and thirsty, and beginning to get weak. I had an instinctive feeling that we needed to keep still to conserve our energy, but my two brothers didn't seem to understand this, and kept jumping around, looking for a way out. There wasn't one, of course – the sack was tied up at the top – and they were just making themselves more and more tired and thirsty. It was hard to breathe, and the two girl kittens were both starting to struggle. Eventually we did all have to lie down quietly because we were too weak to do anything else, even to cry.

We lay there for a long time, maybe hours, maybe days, listening to each other's shallow breathing getting fainter.

And then there was a sound outside – a loud sniffing sound – and the sack was being nudged backwards and forwards. By now I was almost too weak and sick to care what happened, but suddenly a new human voice was calling out:

'What have you got there, Rupert? Leave it alone, boy. Here! Sit! Stay!'

And then there was light, so sudden and so bright, I had to close my eyes, only for them to fly open again with fright at the terrible noise that came next. Have you met any dogs yet, little kitten? Believe me, you need to give them a wide berth. Some of them are quite friendly to cats, others are complete psychopaths who would kill us as soon as look at us. But the main problem with them is, they're loud and excitable. Their humans have to tie them onto long straps just to keep them under control, and if they're unstrapped, they go berserk, running around in circles, shouting their heads off, chasing anything that moves, even though they never seem to catch anything. Well, this was my first introduction to a dog, and it was terrifying. The minute his human had opened our sack, this dog got his nose right inside it and let out a cacophony of horrendous shouting. The human was shouting too, telling him to shut up and sit down, and eventually the dog's face was replaced in the opening of the sack by the human's face. After my experience with the first human I'd ever met, you can imagine how I felt about seeing another one – and this one's voice was just as loud as the first.

'Kittens!' he yelled, staring down at us. I tried to give a little cry of fear, but nothing would come out, and I wasn't the only one – none of my siblings seemed to be able to raise a squeak, either. 'Half dead by the look of 'em. Poor little beggars. Who the hell would dump a bag of kittens in the middle of a field like that? Criminal, that's what it is. Well, I'd better take 'em somewhere, though I reckon it's probably too late to save 'em. Come on, Rupert – let's go, boy. Back to the car. You'll have to have your walk later.'

With that, we were hoisted up in the air again and I was tumbling on top of my poor sisters and brothers, all of us too weak to care. I was barely conscious as I felt the sack being put down again. But a few minutes later, there was an even louder noise, if possible, than the din the dog was still making, and I lay there quaking and shivering, sure it must be the end of the world. I've since worked out that we were in a car, and the noise – I've heard it lots of times since, of course – was the car waking up. They roar at the top of their lungs at first, and then settle down to a kind of loud purr as they run along. It's horrible being inside one, at the best of times – you can feel the vibrations of their tummies rumbling, and they make all sorts of horrible noises, stopping and starting and sometimes screeching. George plays music inside his car now if he has to take me out in it, and that helps a bit. But I shudder to think how scared I must have been back then, in the blackness of that sack, with no idea what was going on. It's probably a good thing my memories of that part are quite dim now.

In fact I don't remember anything else until I found myself being lifted out of the sack. I could hear the human who owned the dog, still talking, and another voice, higher

<del>100</del>

and softer, but my brain couldn't interpret what they were saying any more. As you know, we cats are born bilingual, able to understand Human as well as Cat, but apparently no humans have ever realised this because, of course, we can't speak it. Didn't you know that, little kitten? Didn't you ever wonder why they don't get annoyed when we completely ignore them? They've come to expect it, so it can be quite useful – we cats don't have to do as we're told, like they expect dogs to.

But by now, I think my brain had almost given up working. I didn't like the high-voiced human picking me up, but she was a lot gentler than the horrible man in the shed. Her voice was comforting compared with the loud booming of the male and the shouting of the dog that was still going on. She gently felt me all over, and the next thing I knew she was dripping milk into my mouth from a little tube. It was heaven. I gasped and almost choked on it, I was so desperate to drink. And then I must have fallen asleep.

Well, the next thing I remember was waking up in a kind of cage, and I was all on my own. I tried to cry, and this time I managed a few pitiful little whimpers. The female human immediately came along and, to my relief, my brain was working again enough to understand her.

'Ah, this one's awake,' she said. 'Hello, little one. Are you feeling better?' She opened the cage and picked me up again. I struggled a bit, but when I saw she had the little tube thing in her hand and was going to give me some more milk, I relaxed. 'That's it, puss,' she purred at me gently. 'Drink up, you need all the nourishment you can get. I think this one's going to make it,' she called to another female standing behind her. And then she laughed. 'He's looking for more. That's a really good sign – he's nuzzling me for more milk. I think we'll have to call him *Oliver*. The boy who asked for more!'

And they both laughed, and although I didn't understand the joke, and although I was really too tired to care what they called me, I must admit I thought it was a very fine name.

I must have spent a long while like that, drifting in and out of sleep, being fed milk whenever I woke up, gradually feeling stronger and eventually managing to get up on my little legs again. When I was finally able to scamper around like a proper kitten, I was allowed out of my cage for short periods to run up and down the room. I still had no idea where I was, but I knew I was being looked after. Several of my baby teeth had come through, and as well as the milk, I was being given tiny mouthfuls of meat to try now. Because I knew how it felt to be starving, I promised myself I'd never refuse anything I was offered.

Day by day, I felt myself growing bigger and fitter. Just as I was getting used to my new routine, I was moved to a different cage. This one was bigger, with room to run around and with my own comfy bed and toilet facilities. The female human had taught me to use a litter box. She'd looked very sad as she told me this was something my mother would have taught me if I hadn't been separated from her. The thought of my mother made me cry, and then I started wondering about my brothers and sisters. I hadn't seen them since I'd been taken out of the sack. I wished I could find them and play with them, but nobody ever mentioned them. I still don't know, to this day, what happened to them. But . . . I think I can guess. I'm not even sure whether the thing about us having nine lives is true, anyway.

Ah, sorry, little kitten. Don't cry. Come on, we're just coming to the nice part of the story. It gets more cheerful now. I'll cut to the end. One day, when I woke up in my little bed, there was a new, strange, male human looking at me through the bars of my cage.

'Hello, little Oliver,' he said. I instantly shrunk back against the edge of the bed, my fur standing on end, and gave a little growl. Male humans were bad news. To be fair, this one was keeping his voice quieter and softer than the others, and his face looked smiley, but how could I trust him?

'Would you like me to get him out for you?' my friend, the female, asked him.

'Yes, please.'

'He's had a very traumatic start,' she said quietly as she unlatched my cage. 'Abandoned before he was weaned – probably at about three weeks or so. We didn't expect him to make it, but he's done really well and he's ready for his first vaccinations now.'

I struggled as she picked me up. I didn't want the male to get me.

'It's all right, Oliver,' she said. 'Don't be frightened. He's a bit nervous of new people,' she explained. 'We think he was probably mistreated before he was dumped.'

'Poor little fellow,' the new human said. 'He's such a beautiful little thing, too.' He seemed so different from the other males, with their loud shouting, and especially that first one with his big rough paws. He gave me a little stroke and although I flinched a bit, it was actually quite nice. 'Would you like to come and live with me, Oliver? I promise you'll never be mistreated again. We'll be best mates, you and me. We're both lonely boys who need a pal, aren't we?'

And despite myself, I found myself purring. It would take me a little while to trust him completely, and when he moved me to my new home he let me live quietly upstairs in his private rooms until I was brave enough to face the customers downstairs. But from our first day together, when he sat me carefully on his lap and told me how his own female had died and left him all alone in the world, and that he'd gone to the Cats' Protection home to find himself someone to keep him company, I knew that what he said was right. We were best mates, destined to spend our lives together and look after each other.

That, little kitten, was how I met my George.

CHAPTER
TEN

OK, well now that I've told you all about my poor sad kittenhood, is it all right with you if I get back to my story about last year? Otherwise we're never going to get to the end of it.

As you've probably gathered, it was starting to be winter by now, and I was never a cat for spending a lot of time outside in the winter. I was lucky to have my two cosy foster homes to sleep in, although it has to be said that Nicky and Daniel's cottage was a bit draughty and they didn't turn the heating on very often. However, I must admit there were times, when Sarah was working on her computer in the study, and the children were at school, when I felt a little bored, and needed to stretch my legs. So I'd have a run down the road and round the corner into the main street, and if I couldn't find Tabby and the others to play with, I'd usually run straight back again.

Of course, if there was a dim-witted pigeon or starling to chase while I was out, so much the better. I'm not a bad hunter, little kitten – I'm small and quick enough to take some of the dozy creatures by surprise. I'll give you some lessons when you're a bit bigger. Usually, back at the pub, if I made a kill I'd take it home and leave it by the back door for George. He didn't seem to like having the gifts taken indoors, for some reason. But obviously, I didn't realise other humans shared this dislike. So the first time

I caught a sparrow for Sarah and Martin, I carried it straight through the cat flap into the house. Nobody was around to present it to, so I thought the best thing would be to leave it in the middle of the lounge, by the coffee table, so they couldn't miss it when they came in. But if I was expecting praise for my hunting skill, I was in for a disappointment.

'What the hell?' Sarah said when she saw the decapitated sparrow on the carpet. 'Oh, Ollie! How could you? Poor bird! And we do *not* want things like this brought indoors, thank you very much.'

I slunk away, feeling very confused and upset. Sarah had sounded cross with me – and yet she'd ended up saying *thank you very much*, so I guessed she must have been pleased with the sparrow but, like George, would have preferred it left outside. And as for *poor bird* – well, it had been a fair fight, and he'd lost. What was wrong with that? I ended up deciding my offering might have been too small. She'd been disappointed. Next time, I'd bring her a bigger bird, but leave it on the front doorstep. She'd like that, for sure.

One day, when it wasn't quite so cold, I was feeling more frisky and adventurous than usual. After setting off from the house, something made me keep on going – up to the top of the main street, where the road runs out of houses and pavements and starts to climb a steep hill. I'd never been up here before, so I slowed down to have a look and a sniff around. But apart from the occasional dollop of smelly horse poo (I've never understood why horses don't clean up after themselves like we do), there wasn't really much to see, until I rounded a bend, and there in front of me were a pair of enormous iron gates, with huge birds sitting on top of them. It took me a minute to realise the birds weren't real. I peered through one of the holes that made up the pattern of the gates, and meowed to myself in surprise. There was a very, very long driveway, stretching away into the distance, and on either side of it were massive lawns of lovely grass, dotted with all sorts of shrubs and trees. Far off at the other end of the driveway was a big house, the biggest I'd ever seen. Feeling too curious to be scared, I squeezed through the gap in the gate and dashed across the lawn to the first little group of shrubs, where I lay quietly for a moment, hoping nobody had seen me. When you're exploring somewhere new like this, little kitten, you have to remember there could be a resident cat who will make short work of seeing you off his territory – or even, worst case scenario, an unstrapped dog. However, everything seemed quiet in this huge garden, so I decided to make the most of it, and spent a pleasant afternoon chasing sparrows and blackbirds and stupid woodpigeons all over the lawns, ducking behind trees and jumping out at them, wriggling under bushes and generally having an exhilarating time. I'd intended picking off one of the black-birds to take home, but eventually I was almost too worn out by all the exercise to walk back and, as you can probably imagine, I fell straight asleep as soon as I was through the cat flap.

The next day, I happened to run into Tabby and his latest female, Suki. I couldn't wait to tell them about my new discovery.

'You're talking about the grounds of the Big House,' Tabby said at once, looking shocked. 'You can't go in there.'

'Why not?' I said. 'I did, and it was lovely. You should try it. We'd have a great time together in there. Is it somebody's territory?'

'Yes, but not a cat's. It belongs to the worst-tempered human in the whole village. I should know. I got chased out of there by him once, and he was waving a stick at me like he wanted to hit me with it. I've never been back and as you know I'm a very brave cat, so it's madness for a timid little thing like you to risk it.'

If he hadn't said that thing about me being *timid*, I'd probably have taken his advice and never gone back there. But it was so embarrassing, being patronised like that in front of Suki. She'd been purring away, rubbing her face against Tabby's and making flirty eyes at him, and when she deigned to give me a glance, it was so disdainful, I'm afraid I snapped:

'Actually I'm not timid at all. I'll have you know I'm famous in the village these days for being as brave as a tiger.'

Tabby laughed. I was beginning to wonder why I was friends with him. He didn't behave like this when Suki wasn't around.

'Oh, really?' he said. 'What did you do? Catch a mouse?'

'No!' I retorted crossly. 'I frightened off a male human, if you must know. A very aggressive one.'

'Yeah? What was he – a little human kitten?' Tabby said, making Suki laugh and rub herself even more amorously against him.

I'd had enough. I turned and stalked away from them, waving my tail crossly as I went. So what if it *was* only a human kitten? I'd still been brave. I'd show that self-satisfied Tabby just how much braver I was than him – I'd go back to the Big House every day if I wanted to, and play there for as long as I liked. Huh! Timid, me? What did he know?

Up to a point, it was true that I was becoming famous in the village, but not necessarily for being brave. Everyone was now aware of my situation, that I was temporarily homeless and in foster care, and when I trotted along the road there was always someone who'd stop, bend down and stroke my head, asking how I was and whether I was missing George. George was very popular with everyone in Little Broomford and I got the feeling they felt a kind of collective responsibility towards me, as their pub cat. This made me feel quite proud, and also helped me realise that most of these people who had tried to stroke and pet me when they came to the pub, and whose advances I'd been afraid of, were actually kind and gentle after all.

It was interesting to see how various people in the village were starting to get together in each other's houses now that the pub and the hall weren't available. That same day, after talking to Tabby and Suki, I was going home past the shop when I noticed two women with prams who were laughing and chatting together as they went up the path

111

of the house next door. One was Hayley, who had the baby called Jack. She caught sight of me and exclaimed to her friend:

'Oh, look, it's Oliver. Hello, Oliver!'

I went closer and did a circuit of her legs. There was a cold wind that day and I'd been in a hurry to get home to the warm, but I was so pleased to see the difference in Hayley, I didn't like to rush off. Before, she'd been so quiet and sad, but now she was smiling and laughing out loud, and even little Jack in the pram sounded like he was making a happy gurgling noise instead of that pitiful mewing.

'It's because of Oliver that I've got some friends in the village now,' she was telling the other female. 'I'm sure he led me here deliberately one day when Louise was outside the shop, and left us to chat to each other. I know it sounds silly, but he seemed so anxious for me to walk this way . . .' she said. She laughed, and shook her head. 'Well, maybe I imagined it. But Louise was sorry too because of the mum-and-baby group not meeting, and we decided to start holding these afternoon get-togethers at each other's houses. And now I've met you, and the others, and I can't tell you how much difference it's made, having friends to talk to about the sleepless nights and the crying and the nappies.'

'Friends who understand,' the other female said, smiling back at her. 'We all need that. Well, Oliver, I'm very grateful to you too.'

And she gave me a little rub of my head and I went on my way, feeling happy and satisfied with myself. Perhaps I was getting a bit *too* pleased with myself, with all this flattery from everyone. But you see, I kept remembering that sneering look on Tabby's face and the haughty way Suki dismissed me, and I was determined that one day *they'd* be jealous of *me*.

Of all my new friends in the village, it was Sarah's family who were the most grateful to me, and I knew that was because of the change in little Rose. She was far more chatty and smiley these days, behaving like any human kitten should – running around the house, giggling at things with her sister, rushing home from the school bus excited about this or that. Apparently the young male called Michael Potts hadn't said another single word to her about Sooty or the accident since I'd attacked him. I heard Grace say to her mother that some other boys from their class had seen the confrontation that day, and teased him afterwards about being frightened of a little ginger cat.

'They said he was a coward because he only picked on little girls like Rose, and when a little cat hissed at him he ran away,' she said. 'He didn't like being laughed at by his friends, so he stays away from Rose now and ignores me too.'

'Good,' Sarah said. 'We have a lot to thank Ollie for, don't we?'

'Yes. And he's going to help the Foxes tonight, too.'

Grace ran over to pick me up and give me a hug, but I was too alarmed by what she'd said, and I yowled and dug my claws into the cushion I was sitting on, refusing to be lifted.

'What's the matter, Ollie?' she said, laughing at me. 'Are you in a grumpy mood today?'

What could she expect, with all this talk about foxes? And, just as I'd feared, a bit later, when I'd been resting peacefully in my favourite chair, the doorbell rang and there was a shout from Grace:

'That'll be them. The Foxes!'

As you can imagine, I was instantly leaping out of the chair and making a dash for the cat flap.

'No!' Rose cried out, seeing me run past her. 'Mummy, don't let Ollie escape.'

I couldn't believe it. The whole family seemed to be in on the plot to bring foxes into the house to eat me up – even Rose! Sarah rushed to lock the cat flap before I could get there, so I turned tail, thinking I could leg it out of the front door when they opened it to let the foxes in. But to my horror, Sarah then shut me in the kitchen, calling out to Grace:

'OK, let them in now. I'll keep Ollie in the kitchen until you've closed the front door and then he can come out.'

Meowing in distress, I crept under the kitchen table and tried to make myself as small as I could against the wall. I could hear children's voices, but no foxes barking yet, although I knew they must be out there somewhere. After a few minutes Sarah came back in.

'Oliver, what on earth's the matter?' she said, bending down and holding out her hand to me under the table. I was cowering on the floor, and low rumbling growls of fear were coming up out of my chest. 'Come on, all the Foxes are here to see you.'

And before I could run again, she'd grabbed me in a paw-lock and carried me into the lounge. I closed my eyes and prepared to say goodbye to the world. How many lives was I down to, even if I believed in that piece of folklore? But all I heard was a chorus of children calling out to me:

'Hello, Oliver!' and 'Oh, isn't he lovely?' and 'Is he asleep?'

I opened one eye slowly, and then the other, and glanced round the room suspiciously. Where were the foxes? I decided to stay clinging onto Sarah until I knew.

The little girls were all laughing.

'Is he scared of us?' one asked.

'He's just a bit shy of strangers,' Grace explained importantly. 'He'll be all right when he gets used to you. Just talk to him quietly but don't rush him or try to stroke him straight away.'

One of the girls came a bit closer to me and bent down to look me in the eyes.

'Hello, little shy Oliver-cat,' she said softly. 'I'm Alice.'

'And I'm Olivia – my name's like yours,' said another.

'I'm Evie.'

'I'm Katie.'

All the children were eagerly introducing themselves, even the couple I'd already met when they came to play before. And then Grace added:

'And we're *all* the Foxes – the best Six in Broomford Brownies!'

I did think it was strange that these nice children would want to call themselves foxes. But perhaps that was why they all dressed in brown. And at least, now I knew it was only *them* and not real foxes coming to play, I could relax.

'We're going to study you, Oliver,' Grace said. 'And you can help us to be the first Six to get our "Friend to Animals" badges.'

'And *I'm* going to be helping you too, girls, with your work for the badge. I want to learn all about it because Brown Owl says I can start training to help lead the pack when the full meetings start again,' said Sarah.

'Oh, Mummy, that's exciting,' said Grace.

'Yes. I've been looking for a new interest, something I can do to help the village community.'

'And it's all because of Ollie. We got the idea of meeting in each other's houses because of him, didn't we?'

'Yes, he's a very special cat,' Sarah said, smiling at me. 'Because of Ollie, it seems lots of people in the village are getting together now. Only this afternoon I heard one of the young mums, Hayley, saying some of the mother-and-baby group have started meeting in each other's houses now. She seemed convinced Ollie had introduced her to two of the other ladies.'

And I purred with pride and happiness. But you know what I've heard some humans saying? *Pride comes before a fall.*

CHAPTER
ELEVEN

The following day, I overheard Sarah telling Martin she'd be going out for the day while the children were at school.

'I'm going to start the Christmas shopping,' she said.

'What?' Martin said. 'It's only the middle of November!'

'I know, but Anne and I are going to have a day in town together and just make a start on it. We'll have lunch out. It'll give us a chance to have a good talk about Brownies, too.'

'Fair enough. I suppose Christmas will come round quickly, like it always does.'

'I know.' Sarah was quiet for a minute. 'I only wish it could be a happier time for our neighbours. Young Nicky isn't even looking forward to it. I don't suppose they'll be buying presents.'

'No. Daniel was telling me they still haven't told her parents their visit's off, either.'

Nicky and Daniel had been getting very chatty with Sarah and Martin. It was nice to see my two sets of carers becoming good friends.

'I've been thinking about that,' Sarah said. 'Mart, couldn't we offer to have Nicky's family to stay here for a couple of nights?'

'What, over Christmas?' Martin said, frowning. 'Won't that be a bit much?'

'I don't see why. We haven't got anyone coming this year, have we? They can spend the day with Nicky and Daniel and just come in here to sleep.' She shrugged. 'We could at least offer. I'd really like to help them out.'

'OK, I guess it'd be a nice offer.' He gave her a kiss and pulled on his jacket ready for work. 'Let's ask them round again this evening, and put it to them then.'

'I'll be out all day today, Ollie,' Sarah said, as if I hadn't already heard. 'I'll leave some dried food down for you in case you get hungry. I'll be back in time for the children.'

I felt fed up and lonely after the door closed behind her. I wasn't in the mood to see Tabby – he'd got really annoying ever since he'd been courting that Suki. I didn't even feel like spending the day asleep. I jumped through the cat flap and wandered down the road, looking for something to do. It was a bright sunny day, but very cold, and I had to do a brisk little trot to keep warm. Before I knew it, I found myself heading up the hill towards the place Tabby had called the Big House. Despite my bravado when I'd been talking about it to Tabby, I hadn't actually been back since my first visit, but now the memory of those huge grounds with all the bushes and trees to run and jump around was tempting me back. I bounded through the big iron gates and, keeping a watchful eye out for scary male humans waving sticks, trotted down the driveway and into a particularly exciting shrubbery where I had a lovely time investigating the scents, jumping over branches and disturbing a few dozy birds who were trying to shelter from the winter cold.

The trouble is, little kitten, playing on your own is never as much fun as it is when there's another cat to run around with or a human to provide entertainment. Oh, I know it's great when you're little like you. You kittens can spend hours just chasing your own tails or jumping at your own shadow – I know, I've been young myself, don't forget. But when you're grown up, running around on your own can get a bit boring after a while. If Tabby was too much of a scaredy-cat and too busy showing off to his girlfriend to come with me, perhaps it wasn't really worth going to the Big House any more. I decided to have one more look around before heading home.

This time, I ventured right up to the house, keeping to the long grass wherever possible in case the bad-tempered man came out. As I've already told you, the house was huge, with red brick walls and great big tall chimneys, the biggest I've ever seen. At the back of the house were lots of very tall windows with crisscross patterns on them. I was attracted to the biggest windows, which looked like they would open out onto the gardens in the nicer weather – because I could see the glow of a lamp in the room beyond, and the flickering of a fire, which reminded me of the nice cosy fire George used to make in the pub.

Another thing I've heard humans say, little kitten, which I could never understand but has always bothered me, is *Curiosity killed the cat.* I'd like to know which cat, and how did he get killed? But nobody has ever elaborated on it.

Well, on this occasion I was feeling particularly curious – downright nosy might be nearer the truth – and I forgot about the possibility of it killing me. I sneaked right up close to those glass doors and stared in. I'd half expected to see the angry man Tabby warned me about, and my little heart was racing with adrenaline as I prepared to do a runner as soon as I caught sight of him. But I was in a very daring mood as well as a nosy one, thinking about the story I'd have to tell Tabby and Suki next time I saw them. Luckily I couldn't see any bad-tempered male in the room, just a female in a kind of white overall, sitting by the fire, holding a book. Her lips were moving, and when I pressed my ear against the glass I could hear her talking, as if she was reading out loud. She kept looking over to the other side of the fireplace and smiling. I turned to see what she was looking at, and at first all I could see was a pink blanket on a sofa. Then I noticed a pale, thin arm resting on the blanket. And as I watched, the blanket shifted slightly and a head popped out from the top of it. It looked like the head of a female, about Grace's age or maybe a bit older, but the face was very pale, with dark rings under the eyes, and where the hair should have been, there was just a plain bare top of the head, like the heads of some of the older males who came to the pub. I felt myself squeaking in surprise, and I was about to run off, but the young female must have caught sight of me because she pulled herself further up out of the blanket and through the glass I heard her say:

'Oh, look, Laura. A pretty cat!'

Well, I was never one to walk away from a compliment. I hesitated, still poised to run, my muscles quivering in anticipation of being chased off the premises. The one in the white overall put the book down, walked over to the window and looked straight at me. For a moment, our eyes were locked on each other, while I waited to be shooed away – but suddenly she smiled, bent down and actually spoke to me through the glass.

'Hello, little cat. Well, yes, you *are* a pretty one, aren't you? I wonder where you come from.'

'He must be so cold out there,' the one on the sofa said.

'You'd think so, wouldn't you? Well, he's got a collar on, and he looks well fed so he must belong to someone in the village.'

'He's come to say hello. Can't we let him come in and get warm by the fire?'

There was a moment of hesitation before the one called Laura replied. 'No, Caroline, I don't think so. You know how your father feels about cats. And it wouldn't be right, anyway – he's got a home to go back to. His family might be missing him.'

'Oh.' The girl laid back down again, looking disappointed. She gave me a little wave. 'Bye bye then, little cat. I wish *I* could have a cat, Laura.'

'So do I, love. But your dad doesn't like them, does he. Now then, let's get back to this story, shall we?'

She went to sit back down again and picked up the book. I stayed for a little while longer, watching, and the girl with no hair gazed back at me as she listened to the story. But then I started to feel too cold, quite apart from having serious worries about the father-who-didn't-like-cats (who, it didn't take much intelligence to work out, was the same as the bad-tempered-man-with-a-stick), appearing around a corner of the building at any moment. I might have been feeling brave, and I'd definitely been feeling curious, but I didn't want to be the cat who got killed for it. I scarpered.

I might not have thought any more about it until the next time I saw Tabby. I'd already got my story all planned out for him, admittedly with a few exaggerations about my bravery. But that evening, Martin invited Nicky and Daniel in again for drinks, and I stayed in the lounge with them, dozing in my hammock on the radiator, listening to their conversation. They were all sounding happy – Sarah because she'd had a good day shopping and said she now had *the Christmas spirit*, whatever that was – and Nicky and Daniel because Martin had made them the offer of putting up Nicky's family over Christmas.

'We can't let you do that,' Daniel had said at once. 'No way!'

'Why not? We've got room,' Sarah said, and Martin was smiling and nodding. 'The two girls share a bedroom. We keep the third one as a guest room, and we've got nobody staying with us this Christmas.'

'The boys could sleep in the little study,' Martin suggested. 'There's an old sofa in there, and room for a camp bed. It'd be a bit cosy, but . . .'

'But it's too much to ask of you,' Nicky said. She looked like she was going to cry.

'You didn't ask,' Sarah pointed out. 'We offered. Honestly, it'd be a pleasure.'

And eventually it was all agreed, and Martin poured out more drinks, and the talk turned to things going on in the village. Once again my heart swelled with pride as they related stories to each other about the meetings being arranged in the various villagers' houses – all of which seemed to be attributed to me.

'I've even heard talk in the shop,' Sarah said, 'that Barbara Griggs, the miserable old woman who lives in the cottage down Back Lane and shouts at everyone, has invited Stan Middleton from across the road to play rummy with her in the evenings since the pub closed, and they've been heard laughing their heads off. And there are empty sherry bottles in the recycling every week.'

'Yes, and apparently Stan's joined the pensioners' club, which he swore he'd never do, because they were all *stupid old women talking about their knitting*, and is letting some of them have their meetings in his house,' Martin joined in. 'And he says it's all because he found Oliver being shooed out of Barbara's garden.'

'Good old Ollie,' Daniel said, when they'd all stopped laughing.

'It's all very well, though,' Martin said, suddenly sighing, 'holding meetings and get-togethers in each other's houses when it's just a few people at a time. But what about all the Christmas parties coming up?'

'They've all had to be cancelled,' Sarah explained gloomily to the others. 'My Women's Institute one has already been called off. And the Brownies' one of course. And the pensioners'. All of them.'

'What a shame,' said Nicky. 'There isn't anywhere else in the village big enough to hold them, I suppose.'

'No.' Sarah shrugged. 'Well, there's only one place of any size, of course – the Big House.' And she laughed, and Martin joined in. 'There's no way anything festive is going to happen *there*.'

'What's the Big House?' Daniel asked.

As you can imagine, I was wide awake by now, listening with great interest.

'Broomford Hall. It's just outside the village, going up the hill towards Great Broomford. Used to be the manor house. The last owner was a kind old chap who used to let us hold the summer fair in the grounds. But the new owner . . .' Sarah smiled and shrugged again.

'Is a downright miserable git,' Martin finished for her. 'He's a widower, apparently, and lives up there all on his own. Doesn't often come into the village, but when he does, he's got a face like thunder and not a *good morning* for anyone. Nobody's ever seen him smile.'

'Oh. Well, *that's* not a possibility then, is it?' Nicky said. 'He doesn't exactly sound like someone who'd be prepared to hold any Christmas parties.'

'No.' Sarah shook her head sadly. 'We're all just going to have to go without our Christmas festivities this year, unfortunately.'

I couldn't help meowing in sympathy, she sounded so gloomy. They all turned to look at me, laughing again.

'And even *you* can't help out with this one, Ollie,' Sarah said.

As I said, I was probably getting a bit too puffed up with pride for my own good. I had this reputation now, it seemed, of being the Cat Who Got People Together. And I felt like I'd been given a challenge. Could I do it? Could I actually become the Cat Who Saved Christmas? I didn't know how, but I was determined to give it a go.

CHAPTER
TWELVE

Although Martin kept complaining that it was only November and 'ages' till Christmas, it seemed like everyone had started talking about it now. The children were getting excited about things like Christmas plays that were going to happen at school and apparently involved them dressing up as shepherds and angels, and Sarah having to make strange costumes out of sheets. Every time they got silly and rowdy, they were warned that Father Christmas wouldn't come unless they behaved themselves. I'd actually heard Grace and Rose whispering together about not believing in this Father Christmas person anyway, so I wasn't sure why they pretended they did. Perhaps it's a bit like us with the Nine Lives story. A legend – part of their culture. I could understand that. Anyway, they still seemed to be excited about him coming, whether they believed in him or not.

All the talk of Christmas was making me feel homesick. When I lived in the pub, Christmas was such a lovely time. George put lots of decorations up, with holly and other greenery all around the fireplace, and a really big Christmas tree in the corner, weighed down with shiny baubles and tinsel and sparkling lights. I can see what you're thinking, little kitten. A tree, indoors – yes, it's what everyone does at Christmas. I keep forgetting next Christmas will be your first time. Well, take a hint from me. When your humans

131

bring the tree indoors, they're going to tell you not to touch it. But then they'll hang all the sparkly things on it, putting temptation right in your way. If they don't want these things played with, they shouldn't hang them there. Believe me, it's almost impossible to resist the urge to jump up and swat those sparkly baubles with our paws. I almost brought the whole tree crashing down when I was a little kitten like you, on my first Christmas. It frightened the life out of me and, after that, George hung the sparkly things higher up on the tree so I couldn't reach them. I still tried, though. Some things just can't be resisted.

It was so pretty and cosy in the pub in the evenings, with all the lights, and the flickering of the fire, and although it was true there were a lot more strange people in the bar, which made me a bit nervous, they were all usually in really happy moods. George used to say it was his favourite time of year. And now I couldn't stop thinking about him, living somewhere far away with his sister and her cat allergy and *without me*. It made me mew sadly to myself as I lay in my chair or on Rose's bed snuggled up with her teddies, and sometimes the girls would stroke me and wonder why I didn't seem very happy, and I wished I could explain.

To take my mind off it all, that week I went every day on my little jaunts to the Big House. I didn't waste time playing in the bushes anymore, or at least, not for more than a few minutes. I ran straight up to the big windows where I'd seen the girl and the woman before. Sometimes they were there again, and the girl called Caroline would call out hello to me and watch me with that sad little smile.

Once or twice, there was nobody in the room so I guessed they must be somewhere else in the house. It was so big, they could have been anywhere. One day I got even braver and trotted round the side of the house and all the way to another big door, with steps going up to it. From the top of the steps I could jump onto a wide windowsill and see into another room. It was a huge room, bigger than the bar in the pub, and it was almost completely empty. I couldn't help wondering what on earth it was for, and why anyone would want a room of that size, especially if they didn't have any furniture to put in it. Humans never fail to surprise me. And then I remembered that conversation about the Big House being the only place large enough to hold a party. It was true. Everyone in the village could probably fit in that one huge room.

I didn't hang around. I was always nervous that the angry man who didn't like cats – or humans, by the sound of it – would turn up and catch me. I couldn't understand why Martin had said he lived there on his own. If that was the case, why were the girl and the woman there? Perhaps they were trespassing, like me, and perhaps I should stay well clear of the whole situation. But something made me go back again the next day anyway.

Sarah seemed to be very busy these days. She was always in the kitchen, making things that smelt lovely and spicy and putting them in the freezer.

'More mince pies for Christmas, Ollie,' she'd say as another batch went in. 'It might still be a long way off, but

I've got so much baking to do, I need to get ahead of myself.' I wondered whether she was expecting to feed the whole village rather than just her little family.

'I'll be hosting a little Christmas lunch for the WI,' she explained one evening to Nicky. 'There's obviously not going to be a formal party this year, so we'll just meet here for sausage rolls and mince pies, and people will bring their own drink. It'll be crowded, but who cares? Why don't you come and join us? It'll be on a Saturday.'

'Oh, but I'm not a member,' Nicky protested.

'Well, I was actually going to suggest you might like to join. It's not like you would imagine. We do lots of interesting stuff, and there are several younger women like yourself. It would help you make friends in the village. I know it's hard when you're at work in the city all week.'

'Oh!' Nicky said again, and she laughed. 'You must have known what I've been thinking. I sometimes wonder whether Dan and I will ever fit in here.'

'Of course you will. Everyone's very friendly. Well, most people are. But you haven't been here long, and you've got no free time to mix with people, have you? The WI meet-ings are usually on Tuesday evenings, and of course as you know, while we can't use the hall, we're meeting in each other's homes. Why don't you come with me one week and see what you think?'

'Thanks, Sarah. Perhaps I will.' She still sounded a little doubtful. 'Although I keep saying I'm going to look for an evening job,' she suddenly blurted out. 'Something temporary.

Bar work, or waitressing. But to be honest, I'm always too tired when I get home from work.'

'And I keep saying I don't want you to do that, anyway,' Daniel said, sounding upset. 'Neither of us should be talking about *second* jobs. *I'm* looking for a *better-paid* job, so that we don't have to.'

There was a silence then, which made the whole room suddenly feel very uncomfortable. Sarah and Martin were fidgeting in their chairs, looking into their drinks, doing little coughing noises.

'What kind of work are you in, Dan?' Martin asked eventually.

'I just work in a shop,' he replied, staring at the floor.

I wondered why he sounded so sorry about it. I'd have thought it'd be great fun to work in a shop.

'It's not just any old shop, it's one of the big stores in the West End,' Nicky protested. 'But they pay their staff peanuts.'

That sounded quite fun, too. Not that I liked peanuts myself, but I'd seen Daniel enjoying them, so I wasn't sure what the problem was.

'It's not exactly my dream job,' Daniel said with a sigh. 'I always wanted to be a car mechanic.'

'Really?' Martin was looking interested. 'Did you train to do that?'

'Kind-of. My dad taught me. We both just liked tinkering around with cars, you know? It was a hobby. We used to fix a few neighbours' cars, and Dad used to say that when I left school he'd set me up in business doing it. So I never bothered with my exams – I was always so sure it was what I was going to do.' He fell silent.

'What happened?' Sarah asked gently.

'Daniel's dad had a heart attack, and sadly he didn't survive,' Nicky answered for him. 'Dan had to get a job – any job – to help his mum.'

'Then Mum got a new boyfriend.' Daniel picked up the story. 'And . . . well, she didn't need me anymore. They actually moved to Spain in the end and I hardly ever hear from them. And of course, I met Nicky.' He gave her a little smile.

'So it's my fault, really,' Nicky said, smiling with her face but not with her voice. 'He's never been able to stop working at the shop and start doing what he really wants to, because first of all we lived with my parents but, well, it didn't work out. And now . . .'

'The cottage next door was the cheapest place we could find to rent anywhere.' Daniel shrugged. 'But it's so far to commute to both our jobs – we just didn't think it through properly. After the rent, nearly all our money goes on the train fares. Nicky had only just finished college when we got together. Her parents warned us we were rushing things. We should have listened.'

'But you wanted to be together,' Sarah said softly. Her eyes looked all wet. 'Of course you did. And I'm sure things will get easier in time.'

'Maybe,' Nicky said, not sounding convinced.

She looked at Daniel, and Daniel looked back at her. There was another one of those silences. I could tell there was something somebody wasn't saying. We cats are good at picking up these things.

'The thing is,' Daniel suddenly blurted out. 'It's going to be even harder now.'

'We weren't going to tell anyone yet, Dan,' Nicky said, looking worried. 'Not till we'd told my parents.'

'I know. But what difference does it make? They're going to be livid. They'll *never* help us out now. They'll blame me, and say we're both stupid, and we should have been more careful. And they'll be right, won't they, let's face it.'

Nicky was crying now. I leapt up onto her lap, purring at her, and she gave me little quick strokes like she didn't even know she was doing it.

'I'm pregnant,' she told Sarah and Martin, in a little quiet voice. 'Three months, now. We didn't mean for it to happen, obviously. I put off getting a test to confirm it, for as long as I could – I kept hoping it was a false alarm. Not that we didn't want children. I love children, I work with them. We wanted them, but not for ages yet. We wanted to get married first, and now we'll never be able to afford *that*.' She sighed and wiped her eyes. 'We just seem to get ourselves into one mess after another.'

'Oh, Nicky.' Sarah got up and came over to put her arms around her. I felt like I was in the way, so I jumped down and went to console Daniel instead, rubbing myself against his legs, but he looked too unhappy to care. 'I must admit I did wonder, when you've kept refusing the wine and drinking orange juice. If there's anything we can do to help . . .'

'Thank you. But there isn't, really. We'll just have to get on with it, won't we? I'll work right up till the last minute, and go back again as soon as I've had my statutory maternity leave. At least I can take the baby with me to work!' she added with a little snort of a laugh.

'Oh yes, you work in a nursery, don't you,' Sarah said. 'Can't you find a job in one that's closer to home?'

'Not paying as much as mine does.'

'It's a really posh place,' Daniel said, giving Nicky a proud look. 'All the rich London people send their kids there. Nicky was the highest-placed student of her year on the childcare course, with distinctions in everything. So she had her pick of the best jobs.'

'Oh, clever you, Nicky.' Sarah was looking thoughtful. 'But, of course, it means paying those train fares.'

'Yes. I know. It's swings and roundabouts, I suppose. On the other hand, if we moved back to London, and rented a flat there, even with those astronomical rents, we might still be no worse off, with only a short bus or tube ride to work.'

'I'd like our child to grow up here, in the countryside, though, Nick,' Daniel said, looking kind of wistful.

'So would I, Dan. But we might not have the luxury of that option,' she snapped.

The evening seemed to have come to an unhappy ending. I gave up trying to comfort them all and went off to my bed in the kitchen.

CHAPTER
THIRTEEN

So they've finally decided on a name for you. They took their time, didn't they? Well, fair enough, I know it's an important decision and I agree, you wouldn't want to be lumbered with something embarrassing like *Tiddles* for instance, just because they rushed into it. So you're going to be *Charlie*. Yes, it's good, I like it. It doesn't quite have the class of *Oliver*, but it's got a certain ring to it and at least it sounds a lot more masculine than *Kitty*. And they're getting you an engraved identity disc like mine? Good. Take it from one who knows – even if you're not going to be a wanderer, you never know when events might overtake you and you might end up getting lost in a wood, like I did. No, don't worry. I'm sure that won't happen to you.

So, Charlie, you want to hear some more of my story, do you? I must say I'm quite gratified by how much of an impression it's making on you. I'm sure you'll be learning a few lessons from my experiences. But I should remind you that I learnt quite an important lesson myself because of all this. I learnt that it's not a good idea to be too proud of your achievements. No cat is invincible. We just end up making fools of ourselves if we think we are.

My problem, as I've already mentioned, was that I was getting a bit too carried away with all the praise from the villagers. It was such a nice feeling, to think that I'd person-ally helped everyone get together with new friends and meet up with their old ones. They were all talking about what a friendly place the village had become since the disaster of the fire. Sarah seemed to be one of the brains behind all the new arrangements, alongside myself of course.

'We need to make more use of the notice board,' she said one evening while the family were having their dinner.

'Notice board?' Martin said, looking blank.

'Yes, the one outside the village hall. It's survived the fire, hasn't it, but nobody seems to have used it since.'

'Well, no, because none of the groups and clubs that met there are meeting now, so they've got no announcements to make.'

'Of course they have!' she interrupted. 'We *all* have. We've all been phoning each other, dropping notes through everyone's doors, emailing people, about whose house we're meeting in each week – when all we needed to do was agree a schedule of dates and venues and put it on the board.'

'Put like that, it sounds obvious,' Martin admitted. 'But these things always need someone to organise them.'

'Well done for volunteering, Mart,' she said, laughing, and then, because he looked so taken aback, she added, 'you can organise the dominoes players at least, can't you? I'll get a rota done for the WI, and help Anne sort out the Brownies. Hopefully other people will soon get the message.'

Apparently they did, because within just a couple of days Sarah was saying the pensioners' club and the mum-and-baby group had both put up lists on the board.

'And there are a couple of other notices,' she added. 'It's like everybody had forgotten about the notice board and now they're all starting to use it again.'

'Good for you, then, love. It's a lot easier than phoning around, isn't it, and not everyone's on email. What are the other notices about?'

'Oh, there's one from Kay – you know, the woman who used to run the nursery? Up till now she's managed to keep going, with as many of the children as possible, running it from her own home in Great Broomford. It's obviously been difficult, though, and two of her staff have found other jobs. So she's closing after Christmas. She says she's really sorry to let people down but she simply can't carry on running it from home for the length of time we're going to be without the hall.'

'What's she doing, then? Will she start up somewhere else? Only I'm just thinking, if she's going to need new staff . . .'

'I know what you're thinking.' Sarah smiled. 'Nicky next door. But you know what she said – she can't earn the money she needs, locally. Anyway no, sadly Kay's decided to call it a day and retire. She's in her fifties and she's got a grandchild of her own, now, apparently, and another on the way. So she wants more time for herself and her own family.'

'Fair enough. Can't blame her. But what about the parents who used the nursery for their kids? There isn't another one anywhere around here, is there?'

'No. And even further afield, they'll all have waiting lists, you can bet your life. I don't know what they'll all do,

Martin. It's so difficult for people, isn't it, when they both have to work. It was only a small nursery, but nearly all the working parents in the village used it, even if only for one or two days a week.'

Another day, another problem for Little Broomford. I didn't like to hear about all these people struggling with the details of their lives. It's strange how humans have so many worries and problems in their lives, little kit—sorry, I mean Charlie – when all we cats have to worry about is getting enough to eat and avoiding horrible things like foxes and unstrapped dogs. If they're so much cleverer than us, you'd think they'd have made their lives easier for themselves rather than harder, wouldn't you.

Although I'd heard my human friends talking about the old female called Barbara who half-murdered me when I chased the birds in her garden, I hadn't been anywhere near her cottage again since that day. But every time her name came up, it seemed to provoke lots of smiles and chuckles, and I gathered she'd had some kind of personality change and was being nicer to everyone. Hard though it was to believe, considering how she spoke to me, to say nothing of picking me up by my neck and threatening me with her spoon, I decided I'd pluck up my courage again, and go to see this transformation for myself.

There was a cold wind blowing again that day. Every now and then the wind blew the dry brown leaves that had fallen off the trees earlier on, up into the air, whirling them around like miniature snowstorms. It made me feel kind of skittish and scampery, and I bounded down the road they call Back Lane and took a running jump up onto Barbara's wall. I could see straight into her front room, and to my amazement, there she was, looking just the same as before with her grey hair piled up on top of her head and her glasses halfway down her nose, but this time she had her mouth turned up in a huge smile. In fact as I watched her, she threw back her head, opened her mouth wide, and I could actually hear her laughing from where I was. Sitting next to her on the sofa, all comfy, with his arm resting along the back of the sofa so that he was almost, but not quite, cuddling her, was the old male from over the road, the one they'd called Stan.

Well, I decided to be *really* brave and get a closer look. The windowsill was just about wide enough to sit on, so after a moment poised on the wall, judging the distance, twitching and preparing my muscles for the jump, the way we do, I leapt neatly across the tiny garden and made a good safe landing. From this new vantage point, I could see that the television was on, and both the old humans had their back paws up on the same stool, and a bright red woolly blanket draped over their legs. There was a bottle open on the little table next to Stan, and they both had glasses in their front paws. As I watched them, they sipped from their drinks and turned to smile at each other.

'It's that cat again!' the female suddenly shrieked, pointing at me through the window. It gave me such a fright, I overbalanced and fell right off the windowsill, which was particularly embarrassing as there was a robin watching from the flowerbed, who was no doubt going to go home and tell his entire family about it. I got straight up onto my paws, of course, and started washing myself frantically to show I didn't care. I kept one eye on the front door, half expecting the old woman to come stamping out waving her spoon again, despite her new cosy smiley appearance. But instead, I gradually became aware of the sound of laughter. Not just the quiet chuckling kind of laughing humans do over some of their television programmes, but absolute roars of high-pitched laughter, louder than shouting. It was both of the old humans laughing out loud together. I stopped washing in surprise, listening to the din. And when it eventually died away, I could hear them muttering together, like they were almost too worn out to talk.

'. . . *watching us cuddling up on the sofa . . .*'

'. . . *probably wanted a glass of our sherry . . .*'

'. . . *no, probably wanted to get under the blanket with us . . .*'

'. . . *you scared him half to death, poor little bugger . . .*'

'. . . *fell off the bloody windowsill!*'

At which, to my intense annoyance, they both began to howl with laughter again. I couldn't imagine what was particularly hilarious about seeing a cat fall off a windowsill. Admittedly I wouldn't have expected any better from the robin, but any decent, caring human would surely have come rushing outside to make sure I wasn't hurt, wouldn't you think?

But as I set off home in a huff, I must say I gradually started to see the funny side of it myself. And to be honest, it could only be good news for me that the old Barbara female seemed to have developed a sense of humour.

'It turns out there's now another use for the notice board,' Sarah told Martin the following day.

'Really? You were right, then – it just took one person to start using it again, and within days everyone's caught on! So what's gone on there now?'

'A suggestion from one of the mums whose child has been going to the nursery. She's said that as most of them only work part-time, and only use the nursery two or three days a week, perhaps they could try to pair up to look after each other's children on the days they don't work.'

'Sounds like a sensible idea.' Martin thought about it for a moment, then added, 'But again, it sounds like it'd be an organisational nightmare. Some probably work Mondays and Wednesdays, others Tuesdays and Fridays and so on. They might not get it to fit.'

'I know. But this mum has started a list of names, and asked others who like the idea to write the days they work and the days they'd be available to look after someone's child. At least it's a start, even if it's only a temporary measure.'

'Yes. Good for her. Hope it works. They could all save the nursery fees, too, that way.'

'Exactly. Very enterprising.' She smiled. 'Our villagers have really been working together since the fire, haven't they? If only we could find a way to reinstate our Christmas parties, a lot of the problems might be ironed out before Christmas.'

'Not for Nicky and Daniel, unfortunately.'

'No.' Sarah was stroking me, absent-mindedly, as she spoke. 'That's another situation even *you* can't solve, Ollie.'

Oh boy. Another challenge. I hadn't even got any further with working out how to save the parties yet. I was going to have my work cut out if I was going to be the Cat Who Saved Christmas. I'd better catch up on my sleep while I had the chance.

CHAPTER
FOURTEEN

With all the humans so busy and caught up in their own worries and plans for Christmas, and making rotas and notices for their meetings, and Tabby being such a pain showing off to his girlfriend, I just carried on with my solitary visits to the Big House. For a couple more days I sat outside the big windows and talked to the girl called Caroline through the glass. I knew instinctively that there was something wrong, because she didn't run around and play like Grace and Rose. She was as quiet as Rose used to be when I first met her, but there wasn't any sign of a damaged paw to explain it. I knew she was always pleased to see me, and the woman called Laura seemed pleased too because it was cheering Caroline up.

'I wish we could let him in,' Caroline would say, but Laura shook her head and reminded her that her father would be cross.

I still hadn't seen any sign of the father, despite Martin and Sarah saying he was the only person who lived there. Obviously they didn't know as much as I did about who lived where in the village. Or perhaps the father was just a made-up person, like this Father Christmas they all talked about.

And then came the day when it was so cold my fur was almost growing icicles. As I stood outside the glass doors meowing to Caroline, something very unusual happened.

Laura went out of the room, and for a few minutes Caroline stayed where she was on the sofa, watching me. Then suddenly she pushed her blanket off and got up. Very slowly and unsteadily, holding onto the furniture, she made her way over to the big doors, turned a key and opened one of them – just wide enough for a little cat like me to squeeze through. All this time she was looking over her shoulder, making sure Laura wasn't coming back. Well, I have to admit I hesitated for a moment. Wouldn't anyone, in the circumstances? But I was so cold, and the fire in that room looked lovely and warm, and Caroline was whispering urgently to me:

'Come on, little cat, quick! Come in while she's not looking.'

And I did. I ran in as fast as my little legs would carry me, dived onto that sofa and huddled under the pink blanket. Despite the fact that my heart was pounding with anxiety, I couldn't help purring at the same time because the blanket was so soft and warm. Caroline took longer to return to the sofa herself. She was breathing hard as if she'd been chasing birds round the garden for hours, and when she sat down and pulled the blanket back over her, I climbed onto her legs and I could feel them trembling. I found her hand and gave it a little lick, and she giggled.

'What are you laughing about?' Laura said as she came back into the room.

I stopped licking, my ears up, on full alert. Was I about to be thrown out?

'Nothing,' Caroline said, giving another little giggle.

'Well, it's good to see you happy. I know you've been bored, but perhaps later this week I'll start putting up the Christmas decorations, and you can watch me.' She stopped, then asked sharply, 'What's that noise?'

Oh dear. I'd started purring again without even realising it. It was hard not to, the warmth and comfort was so lovely after being outside in that icy cold.

'Just my tummy rumbling. Sorry,' Caroline said, giggling again.

'Are you hungry? Well, that's a good sign. Shall I just finish reading you this story, and then get you some soup?'

'Yes please.'

There was a rustle of pages, and Laura started to read. It was a story about some Dalmatian puppies. It was quite exciting and I was just starting to get into it when she suddenly broke off and said, 'The little cat went away again, then?'

'Yes,' Caroline said, giving me a little nudge with her arm. I snuggled up closer to her and licked her hand again, and I could feel her trying not to laugh.

'What are you grinning about now?' Laura said, with a smile in her voice.

And then I made my big mistake. I was so enjoying my cuddle with Caroline, I climbed right on top of her tummy and started doing the turning-around-and-pawing thing. And I was purring again. I knew it, I just couldn't help it.

'What's that?' Laura said more sharply.

And of course, the next thing I knew, the blanket was being pulled off us both and Caroline was saying, 'Sorry, Laura. He just looked so cold, and he's so cute.'

Needless to say, I'd jumped off the sofa as soon as I felt the blanket being lifted. I ran to the big window and stood by it, yowling my head off. If there'd been another door open, I'd have run out of it by now, without even thinking about where I might end up. I think I'd even have run up the chimney if there wasn't a fire in the grate.

But suddenly, in between my frantic yells of fear, I realised I could hear Laura laughing.

'All right, all right, little cat,' she said, coming over to me and bending down. 'I'm not going to hurt you.' She gave me a stroke and looked at the disc on my collar. '*Oliver*,' she said. 'What a nice name.'

I stopped yelling and glanced over at Caroline. She was smiling back at us.

'I thought you'd be cross,' she said to Laura.

'And I certainly should be. But between you and me, I can't see the harm in it. He's a lovely friendly little thing. He obviously likes you, doesn't he – coming back every day like this. Well, you'd better not breathe a word of this to your father, all right? Or I'll be in big trouble. And you really shouldn't have got up and walked across the room without me helping you. You're still very weak. You could have fallen over.'

'I was careful.'

'Good. Well, perhaps I should be pleased that you managed to find the strength in your legs to do it. Now,

I'm going to heat up your soup, and if you want me to keep Oliver's visits our little secret, you'd better promise me you'll try to eat it all up.'

'I promise. Thank you, Laura,' Caroline said. 'Can Oliver come back on my lap?'

'After you've had the soup. I'm not being responsible for you spilling it and scalding yourself, on top of everything else.'

With that, she gave me another little stroke before she went back out of the room. Some humans just can't help themselves – they just love us cats, even if they pretend not to. I lay down on the rug in front of that lovely warm fire, and Caroline talked to me in her quiet gentle voice, telling me how much she wished she could have a little cat of her own. Laura brought in a bowl of something steamy for Caroline, on a tray, and to my surprise, a bowl of milk for me, which I lapped up enthusiastically. And when we'd both finished, she picked me up and put me on the blanket with Caroline, who was having a nap. I turned around a few times, settled myself down, and was so contented I dozed off almost immediately, all thoughts of angry cat-hating fathers banished from my mind.

After that, whenever I arrived at the big window, Laura let me in, and together we'd entertain Caroline with one of the usual games so irresistible to us cats – balls being rolled across the floor (and under the sofa) for me to chase, feathers being used to tickle me and get me rolling on my back with my paws in the air, strings dangled to make me jump up on my back legs – all giving me some good exercise and getting Caroline laughing her head off at the same time. Then we'd have our refreshments, and finally I'd be allowed to snuggle down with Caroline while we both had our naps. When she woke up, Laura would let me out of the door again and I'd scamper back to my foster home.

The second time, on my way back I ran into Tabby. For once, he was on his own – no sign of Suki anywhere – so I stopped to say hello.

'You'll never guess where I've been,' I said, desperate to show off my news.

'Go on. Where?' He didn't sound overly interested.

'The Big House. I go there every day now.'

'You're more of a fool than I thought you were, then,' he snapped. 'I warned you to stay away from there, didn't I? You'll end up being beaten with a stick by the angry man, and then you'll be sorry.'

'No, listen, it's not like that at all,' I insisted. 'There isn't any angry man. He must be a myth, like Father Christmas.'

Even as I was saying this, there was a little voice in the back of my head reminding me of the things Laura had said about Caroline's father. But I ignored the little voice. I didn't want to believe it.

'Father Christmas isn't a myth,' Tabby retorted. 'Who told you that?'

'The human kittens at my foster home. They say he isn't real, but they pretend to believe in him, so they can still have presents.'

'That's rubbish. You'll believe anything, Ollie. You're so naïve.'

'No I'm not! I'm telling you, I've been to the Big House loads of times now, and there's no angry man there. There's just a woman called Laura and a girl with no fur on her head who lies on a sofa.'

'Oh, for mewing out loud, Ollie. Have you been at the catnip again? You're either seeing things, or you've got a very active imagination.'

'I've been inside now,' I shouted at him. 'They play with me and give me milk, and I snuggle up with the girl on the sofa. Laura says I'm cheering her up.'

'Yeah, right. Pull the other paw,' he said disdainfully. 'If you've got any sense, you'll stop going there, and that's all I'm saying on the subject.'

I was furious with him for not believing me. What was the matter with him, anyway? He looked like he'd just been told he had an appointment at the vet's.

'You're in a bad mood, aren't you?' I said. 'Where's Suki? Has she dumped you?'

There was a long silence. He was looking the other way, making little growly noises in the back of his throat. I wasn't sure if he was about to snap my head off, or burst into mews.

'What?' I demanded again. '*Has* she dumped you, then?'

I mean, fair enough, I'd try to be sympathetic if he was really upset. I'd never had relationships with females myself, but it seemed to matter enormously to Tabby. And although he'd been mean to me recently, we had been friends for a long time.

There was another silence. I was just about to give up and walk away, when he said, in a strangled kind of voice:

'I wish she *had* dumped me, Ollie. If only she had, before we got so – you know – carried away with each other.'

I *didn't* know, to be honest. I counted myself lucky that George had taken me to the vet when I was a kitten and *got me done*, as they called it. From what I'd seen, having relationships with females only ever led to trouble, to say nothing of the kind of stupid showing-off behaviour I'd seen in Tabby recently. Why would I want to bother with it? But I gave him a little head-rub of sympathy, even though I had no idea what he was on about.

'You really don't get it, do you, Ollie?' he said. 'You're not a victim of your hormones like I am.'

Well, thank goodness for that. It sounded most uncomfortable.

'She hasn't *dumped* me,' he went on, looking like all his nine lives were over. 'She's *pregnant*. She's going to have kittens. She's saying it's my fault, and now she keeps on moaning and complaining about it. It's putting me right off her, to be honest. I mean, she's a nice-looking cat, but I can't stand all this bad-tempered yowling – I have to turn tail and run away from her when she starts. Know what I mean, Ollie?'

I didn't. But as I did my best to comfort him, I'm ashamed to say all I could think about was that maybe now he'd stop being such a pain in the neck and be my friend again.

CHAPTER
FIFTEEN

So I now had human friends *and* cat friends who were expecting babies – and none of them seemed very happy about it. By the way, Charlie, I noticed you looking a bit apprehensive when I mentioned George taking me to the vet's for that little operation. Honestly, it wasn't because George was being cruel to me, even though at the time I admit I was frightened out of my life.

'Ollie,' he said in his kind, reassuring voice, 'I'll never know exactly what happened to you when you were very tiny, but when you were handed in to the people at the Cats' Protection League, you were starving, and lucky to be alive.'

You can imagine how I shuddered to be reminded of this, but he quickly went on:

'Your mother was probably a stray who had lots of kittens and, sadly, whoever found you and your brothers and sisters didn't want you. There are lots of poor stray cats in the world, Ollie, all of them homeless and hungry and having lots of unwanted kittens that nobody looks after. If I didn't have you neutered, we'd just be adding to the problem. It wouldn't be your fault – you'd just be following your instincts. But I want to be a responsible cat owner, and do what's right.'

At the time, although I was moved by what he said, I didn't fully understand. But I loved George and knew he would never do anything to hurt me. And it's never

161

bothered me, about having girlfriends. What you've never had you've never missed. So if your humans make the same decision for you, don't be frightened. Look at me – I've turned out fine, haven't I?

It was different for my human friends, Nicky and Daniel, of course. Humans tend to stay in their pairs, and keep their human kittens with them and bring them up together. Well, so I've been led to believe, although it doesn't always seem to work out that way. It seems a good arrangement when it works out well, though, and because Nicky and Daniel were such nice humans, who obviously loved each other, I was sure they would stay together and be good parents if only they weren't so worried about money.

One afternoon, as I passed the place outside the village shop where the pram-pushing females always stopped to chat, I overheard the one called Louise saying:

'It's all very well, this idea of looking after each other's children after Kay's retired. But I work five mornings a week. Everyone else who works part-time seems to do two or three whole days, so there's no one available to cover all the hours I work. I've asked my boss if I can change to a different arrangement, but it's no good – he specifically needs me in the office every day. He says I could do less hours each day if necessary, but that wouldn't help at all. I'd still have no one to look after Freya and Henry, and I'd be earning less money.'

'What are you going to do?' Hayley asked her.

'I have no idea. I'm worried I might lose my job. My mum might be able to come over a couple of days a week, but it's asking a lot. She doesn't drive and it's a long way on the bus. I've written an advert, actually, appealing for a nanny. I couldn't afford a live-in one, and anyway it'd only be for twenty hours a week.' She waved a piece of paper at her friends. 'I'm just going to put it on the notice board. But I doubt I'll have any luck. I can't think of anyone suitable in the village.'

'No. Maybe you should advertise in the local paper. You might get someone from Great Broomford, or one of the other villages,' one of the other women said.

'Yes. I'll do that. Thanks.'

Louise went off with her pram, looking tired and worried. I followed her to the notice board and watched as she pinned her paper up.

'Oh, hello, Oliver,' she said, almost tripping over me as she turned back to the pram. 'How are you?' She bent down and gave me a little stroke. I didn't mind. I'd got used to the pram ladies. 'I wish I had your life. No worries, just a nice warm bed and someone to feed you. Lucky old you.'

Actually I could have argued with that. After all, I'd been through enough worries and trauma to last me all nine lifetimes, hadn't I. But it was true that I was quite comfortably off these days and was certainly beginning to be aware of how difficult life could be for some humans. I walked round her legs, giving her a little head rub to console her, before scampering off after a couple of sparrows who'd caught my attention, hopping about under a nearby hedge.

*

That same evening, Sarah and Martin were talking about Nicky and Daniel again. They obviously so badly wanted to help them, and I really wished there was something I could do, too.

'I know the local mums are getting this child minding rota organised,' Martin said. 'But are you *sure* there isn't anyone in the village who might prefer to *pay* someone – someone well-qualified like Nicky – to look after their kids?'

'Not as far as I'm aware,' Sarah said with a shrug. 'And I'm not being funny, but not many people around here really know Nicky yet, let alone know she's a nursery carer. If she comes to a WI meeting, I can introduce her to people and perhaps everyone can put the word about for her, but you know what she said – she earns top dollars at that nursery in London and . . . what is it, Ollie? Do you want to go outside? Go on, then, the cat flap isn't locked.'

Sometimes, Charlie, I wish so badly that we could talk Human as well as being able to understand it. It can be so frustrating wanting to tell people something important, when all they can think of is our toilet requirements!

I waited till the next time I saw Daniel outside the cottage. It must have been a Saturday because he was carrying the rucksack he brought me home in that very first day, and was heading off towards the woods, whistling. He always did that when he went hunting for firewood. I think he enjoyed it, a bit like us hunting mice, but easier of course because humans are pathetic hunters.

'Meow!' I said to him. 'Meow, meow, meow!' I tried to make it sound as urgent as possible.

He stopped and looked at me. 'What's up, Ollie? Didn't any of us give you your breakfast this morning?'

Honestly, if it isn't our toilet requirements, it's our stomachs. I suppose we should be grateful, but don't they realise we do occasionally have thoughts that *don't* concern our bodily functions?

'MeOW!' I shouted at him, and stalked down the road a few paces in front of him, twitching my tail and looking back to see if he'd got the message.

'You want to come to the woods with me, boy?' he said, still standing on the spot staring after me.

No, for mewing out loud, I'm going in the opposite direction, I thought with exasperation.

'You want *me* to come with *you*?'

At last! Finally, he caught up with me and I bounded ahead to where the notice board stood outside the wreck of the village hall. I have to say, it took several frustrating minutes of walking round and round the posts supporting the notice board, several walks around Daniel's legs and then back to rub my head against the posts again, before he started looking at the notices.

'Domino team meetings, next venue TBA,' he read out loud. 'Pensioners' afternoon tea at Barbara Griggs's house. Cub Scouts' cook-out in Clive and Beryl's garden, please bring own sausages.'

Further down! I wanted to shout.

'Mums-and-babies group – next meeting at Hayley's house Tuesday 2pm, we will sing nursery rhymes, bring shakers. Shakers?' he asked himself, looking puzzled. Then: 'Child minding rota. As you know Kay's nursery business is closing 31 December. Please add your availability and requirements. Oh yes. That's what Sarah and Martin were telling us about. And what's this? Louise and Dave Porter require kind, qualified person to care for Freya, three, and Henry, eighteen months, twenty hours per week, Monday to Friday mornings, payment by agreement. Apply to . . . Wow, Ollie. This might be right up Nicky's street. Lucky I saw it, eh?' He gave me a funny look then. 'If it wasn't a ridiculous thing to think, I could almost believe you knew this was here.'

He did actually try to tell Nicky it was because of me that he'd seen it, but she just laughed. Unfortunately, she also laughed when he told her what the notice had said, but it wasn't the kind of laugh that sounded as if she was really amused. In fact she sounded quite snappy about it.

'Don't be ridiculous, Dan. Twenty hours a week, on local wages? How's that supposed to be a good idea? We wouldn't even be able to pay the rent, let alone feed ourselves.'

'You wouldn't have to pay train fares,' he reminded her. 'And I wouldn't have to be worried sick about you getting exhausted from commuting, closer to when the baby's due.'

'Nobody's asking you to worry about me,' she said crossly. 'Just go and find some firewood, please, Dan, and stop coming up with stupid ideas.'

He picked up his rucksack and went off towards the woods again, only this time he wasn't whistling. And I slunk away to have a sleep in their kitchen, feeling sorry that I'd tried to help. Maybe I wasn't as clever as I thought I was. The cat who saved Christmas? At the moment I just seemed to be the cat who caused arguments.

At least the atmosphere in Sarah and Martin's house was more cheerful. On that same Saturday, the whole family went out in the car and came back laughing and excited, with a tree strapped to the car roof. Of course, from my Christmases at the pub, I knew straight away what it was, but Sarah must have thought I was a silly little inexperienced kitten like you, because she picked me up and cuddled me as Martin carried the tree inside, telling me not to worry, it wasn't going to hurt me. I felt quite offended, but at the end of the day there was no point in passing up the opportunity for a nice cuddle.

'Can we decorate it now, Daddy?' Grace was shouting as she danced around the room. '*Please*, Daddy, can we . . .'

'No. Let's leave that for a few days, at least. It's still far too soon – I don't know why I let you talk me into buying one when it's not even the first of December until Monday.'

'Oh, Daddy, *please*! Now we've got it, can't we put the decorations on?' She was jumping up and down and going red in the face.

'Calm down, Grace,' Martin said. 'I've said no.' He gave Sarah a look, and nodded at Rose, who was sitting quietly on the sofa, just watching Martin trying to prop the tree up in its bucket.

'Dad's right,' Sarah said. 'It won't hurt to wait a few more days for the decorations.'

'Oh, *Mum!*'

'You can both do it together, after Rose has her plaster off on Thursday,' she said.

'Oh.' Grace looked at her sister. 'Why? She can help me now, with her good arm, can't she?'

'That's not very fair, is it? It'll be much nicer if you can both do it together, and she'll manage a whole lot better when she's got both arms free.'

'But you said they might not even take the plaster off when she goes to the hospital on Thursday,' Grace said, crossly. 'Then we'll *never* be able to put the decorations up.'

'We hope it *will* come off.' Sarah sounded equally cross now. 'But if it doesn't, we'll do the decorations on Thursday evening anyway, and *I'll* help Rose so that she can join in properly.'

'It's not fair,' Grace moaned.

'And it's not like you to be so selfish, Grace,' Martin snapped at her. 'Rose has had to put up with doing everything one-handed all these weeks and hasn't complained about it. Think yourself lucky it wasn't you that got hurt.'

'I wouldn't have been stupid enough to run into the road,' Grace retorted – and then she went suddenly even redder, and put her paw over her mouth. 'Sorry!' she gabbled. 'I didn't mean it!'

But she was too late saying sorry, because Rose had burst into tears, and Sarah had put me down abruptly, got hold of Grace by the shoulders and marched her quite roughly out of the room.

'Go upstairs and stay there until you've had time to think about what you just said,' I heard her saying angrily. 'I know you're overexcited about the Christmas tree, but that was a really nasty thing to say to your sister. And to think you were the one sticking up for her when other children were being unkind.'

'I know, I'm sorry, I didn't mean it!' Grace was still saying through her sobs as she went upstairs. 'I'm sorry, Rose,' she called back from their bedroom.

But Rose was crying quietly on the sofa, and Martin was muttering to himself that if Grace carried on like that she wouldn't get any Christmas presents. The whole day seemed spoilt.

I jumped up on Rose's lap and snuggled up to her, giving her good paw a few licks of consolation.

'I'm *not* stupid,' she said in a little quiet voice as Sarah came back into the room. 'I only ran into the road because I loved Sooty.'

'Grace knows that really,' Sarah told her, joining us on the sofa and putting an arm round Rose. 'She was just being spiteful. She probably resents the extra attention Rose has had,' she added quietly to Martin, who sighed and nodded.

When Rose had stopped crying, I jumped down and ran upstairs to see Grace. She was lying on her bed, looking like she'd cried even harder than Rose. Her face was swollen and blotchy and her eyes were all red.

'Oh, Ollie!' she said, picking me up and cuddling me. 'I wish I hadn't been so horrible. I don't know what's the matter with me. Am I turning into a horrible person?'

'No!' I mewed at her in Cat. I didn't really know what else to say.

'I do love Rose, and I actually think she was really, really brave to try to save Sooty,' she said, her eyes starting to fill up with tears again. 'She was just getting over it all, wasn't she, and now I've gone and upset her all over again. How can I make it up to her?'

I didn't have any answers. I just purred against her neck to show I understood.

She jumped up suddenly, wiping her eyes, opened the drawer in her bedside table and pulled out a little pink purse, which she unzipped and tipped upside down on the bed. Lots of brown coins, a few silver ones and one of those pieces of paper they call *five pound notes* fell out, and she started counting it all up.

'I know what I'll do,' she said, sounding excited again. 'I'll use all my money to buy Rose a new cat of her own, to keep. She can call it Sooty again. *That*'ll make her happy, won't it, Ollie?'

I nearly fell off the bed. A new cat? Another Sooty, a permanent member of the family, coming to live in my foster home? I'm sorry to say, Charlie, the selfishness problem must have been catching that day, because all I could think was *What about me?*

CHAPTER
SIXTEEN

CHAPTER
SIXTEEN

For a few days, things were more settled in Sarah and Martin's house. But I was so worried about the suggestion of a new cat, I decided I'd better try harder than ever to make myself irreplaceable. Since being told off for leaving the headless sparrow in the lounge, I'd tried leaving a few gifts of mice and birds by the back door, but Sarah hadn't seemed particularly thrilled. So this time, I spent a while stalking the stupid pigeons who dominated the bird feeder a few gardens down the road. They're not particularly hard to catch, but they're big and cumbersome to carry off. I chose the biggest, plumpest one, and just to make sure it was properly appreciated, left it on the front doorstep.

Sarah was indoors, working in the study. I went in to keep her company, jumping up on the desk next to her computer.

'Hello, Ollie,' she said, but she seemed to find the screen of the computer more interesting than me. I tried to lie across the part where she tapped out writing – it was nice and warm from her hands – but she sighed and lifted me off. I really didn't feel very welcome. Was she getting bored with me? I toyed for a few minutes with a funny-shaped thing lying next to the computer, but then she reached for it herself and sighed again.

'Ollie, please don't play with the mouse,' she said, sounding tired and fed up.

Mouse? I stared at it. If it was a mouse, it had been dead for a long time, that was for sure.

'I'm very busy,' she said. 'This is a tricky piece of work and I need to concentrate. I think you'd better get down.'

And she lifted me off the desk, putting me down quite firmly on the floor. I was mortified. She *must* be getting bored with me! Was I going to be expelled from the family even sooner than I'd feared? I slunk off to my bed in the kitchen and curled up tight, burying my head under my tail, and consoled myself with a little nap.

When I woke up, there was pandemonium in the house. The children were home from school, they were both shrieking at the tops of their voices and Sarah was trying to calm them down.

'It's *gross*,' Grace was shouting. 'I nearly *trod* on it.'

'Its eyes were staring at me,' Rose cried. 'It's horrible.'

'Why does Ollie do it?' Grace said. 'I wish he wouldn't. Sooty never did it, did he, Mummy?'

I sat up in bed, horrified. What had I done wrong? I tried my best to please them, and I just got compared unfavourably with Saint Sooty. How could I compete with a ghost?

'Sooty *did* do it,' Sarah said calmly. 'You don't remember, because you were too little when he was a young cat. He got too old to hunt in the end. All cats like to hunt – it's normal. I agree, it's not very pleasant for us, but it's part of living with cats, and there's no point making all this fuss. I'll clear it up. Now, calm down, and go and get changed out of your uniforms.'

I stayed in the kitchen, sulking, feeling unappreciated. A little while later, both girls came in to talk to me.

'I know you can't help it, Ollie,' Grace said very seriously, squatting down to stroke my head. 'But really, it isn't very nice.'

'Next time, Ollie, leave it somewhere else,' said Rose. 'A long way away.'

'Yes, as far away as possible,' Grace said, and they both giggled.

At least they didn't seem cross with me anymore. I sighed. Humans could be *so* hard to understand at times.

The next day, Sarah took Rose to the hospital and they both came home with big smiles on their faces.

'Look, Ollie!' she shouted, running into the room, waving both paws at me. 'My plaster's off! I can cuddle you properly now. Can we do the decorations now, Mummy?'

'Yes, when Grace gets home from school,' Sarah said. 'I don't want any more arguments about it.'

There was a much better atmosphere in the room this time, with both girls happy and excited about climbing on a chair to put the sparkly stuff and the shiny baubles on the tree.

'You can put the angel on the top, Rose,' Grace said. She'd been particularly kind to her sister since the trouble at the weekend. 'I'll hold the chair steady for you. Be careful you don't fall.'

Nothing more was being said about a new cat. But as I'm sure you can imagine, I had my ears up constantly, listening for any talk about one replacing me. It had brought home to me how precarious my position was, as a foster cat in the family. Thank goodness I'd got a back-up with Nicky and Daniel next door, even though I suspected they might prefer their new baby to me when it arrived. Oh, how I wished I could be back in my pub, where I had George all to myself and didn't have to compete with anyone else.

I tried to console myself with the new friends I'd made at the Big House. It was so nice to see Caroline looking so happy when I arrived, and in fact the next time when Laura let me in and gave me her usual little cuddle before putting me on Caroline's lap, she said:

'You're doing Caroline so much good, you know, Oliver. You've really cheered her up since you've been coming here. I can't see how Julian could possibly object.'

I guessed Julian must be Caroline's father. It was good to hear that he couldn't object to me. I decided now that he couldn't be the same person as the angry man with the stick that Tabby had gone on about. I'd still never seen any sign of the father, and I guess I was getting a little bit complacent. I'd stopped looking over my shoulder when I ran up the driveway and meowed at the glass doors. I should have known it was too good to be true.

It happened on another Saturday, the one after the argument about the Christmas tree. Looking back, I suppose until then I hadn't been going to the Big House at weekends, because there was always so much more going on at my two foster homes. Daniel and Nicky were at home, Martin and the children were around, and sometimes the Brownie Foxes turned up to do their important study of my behaviour. Having so many people to play with, I didn't get bored and lonely like I sometimes did during the week. But now I'd started seeing Caroline every day, and because Laura had told me I was doing her good, I didn't want to miss out any days anymore.

I bounded down the drive as usual and called out to Laura from my normal place at the glass doors. For a minute I thought nobody was there. I put my ear against the glass and heard Caroline calling out to Laura: 'Oliver's here!' She sounded a bit startled.

'Oh!' Laura had rushed back into the room and was staring at me in surprise. 'He's never come at the weekend before. We'd better not let him in,' she said, looking back over her shoulder. 'It *would* have to be one of the Saturdays that your dad works from home.'

'Oh, *please*, Laura!' Caroline said.

'Yes, *please*, Laura!' I meowed in Cat. It was cold outside.

'Just for a little while? I can keep him under my blanket,' Caroline was pleading. 'Daddy's in his study. He'll be in there all morning, won't he?'

'Well . . .' Laura sighed, looked back through the door of the room again, then quietly closed it behind her. 'All right, then, but only for a few minutes. If he makes any noise, he'll have to go straight out again.'

She opened the glass door for me and I dashed over to the sofa and jumped up next to Caroline. She giggled and pulled me onto her lap, putting the blanket right over me.

'No noise, Oliver,' she whispered. 'You've got to be a very quiet, very *secret* cat today.'

I quite liked the idea of being a secret cat. It wasn't easy to keep from purring, though, snuggled up like that under the warm blanket with Caroline giving me a nice stroke.

'Can we have the TV on?' she asked Laura. 'Then if Oliver does start meowing, Daddy won't hear.'

'OK.' Laura smiled at her. 'Just this once.' I heard the television being turned on and for a while, I settled down and closed my eyes, enjoying the warmth and comfort and letting Caroline's stroking soothe away my worries about being displaced by a new Sooty.

'I'm just going to the bathroom, Caroline,' I heard Laura say after quite a while. 'And when I come back, Oliver's going to have to go. No fuss, please, otherwise he'll have to stop coming altogether.'

'OK,' Caroline said reluctantly. 'Sorry, Oliver,' she whispered to me as the door closed quietly behind Laura. 'She's worried about my dad, you see. Maybe I should get brave enough to tell him about you, but since I've been ill he tends to get upset about things.'

There was the sound of the door opening again. Laura coming back, I supposed. I made the fatal mistake of getting up and having a stretch, before turning round to settle myself back down again. To my surprise, Caroline pushed me down quite hard under the blanket, giving a little gasp.

'Daddy!'

I froze. I had a horrible feeling my tail was half out of the blanket. A frightened little mew escaped from my lips.

'What the hell?' came this loud, cross voice. Footsteps thumped across the floor. The blanket was lifted off us, and a huge paw grabbed me round the back of my neck. I was suddenly reminded so horrifyingly of being grabbed in the same way by that very first scary man in my life, when I was only a tiny kitten, that I screeched in terror and dug my claws into the skin of the man's other paw.

'Ouch! Let go, you horrible, vicious thing.' He flung me off himself and I landed, shaking with fear, on the floor near the glass door.

'Let me out! Let me out!' I cried out to Caroline in Cat, but even if she could have understood me, she was too busy crying herself.

'Daddy, you didn't have to do that. You've hurt him.'

'I'll hurt him a lot more if I ever see him in this house again. What on earth was Laura thinking of, letting you have an *animal* in here with you? LAURA!' he shouted – and she came running in, red in the face and trembling almost as much as I was.

'I'm sorry, Julian. I didn't think it'd do any harm – he's a nice clean little cat, he has a collar on . . .'

'I wouldn't care if he had a dinner jacket on. You know perfectly well I do not allow *animals* in my house, and especially not on my daughter's sickbed.'

'It's not a sickbed, Daddy, it's a sofa. I'm not as sick as I was, I'm getting better,' Caroline cried.

'You're still susceptible to germs, you know that. Your immunity is low. You're not supposed to mix with *people*, never mind dirty, flea-ridden *animals*.'

Flea-ridden? If I hadn't been in a state of such abject terror, I'd have jumped up and clawed him again for being so rude.

'Julian, I really think you're overreacting,' Laura started to say, but he turned on her angrily.

'Overreacting? Can I remind you that this is my *daughter*, my only child, the only person I have left to care about in my life? Wasn't it enough that she had to have this bloody awful illness and go through months of treatment that made her sick and weak and . . .'

'And she's *getting better*, Julian. Yes, she's still weak, but she's getting stronger every day. You've got to stop treating her like an invalid. She wants to make friends, she needs company. It's only people with colds and germs she needs to keep away from, not everybody. She was going crazy with boredom until Oliver started visiting.'

'*Oliver*? That *animal*? You mean to tell me this has been a regular occurrence – he's been coming here all the time, encouraged by you, behind my back?' For a minute I thought he was going to grab hold of Laura by the neck like he did with me, but Caroline spoke up.

'It's not Laura's fault, Daddy. I *made* her let him in. It's true, I was bored. It's been lovely seeing Oliver every day. I feel better because of him.'

The man just ignored her, though, and carried on shouting at poor Laura.

'I employ you to *care* for my daughter, not to put her health at risk by letting *cats* into my house. Do you understand?'

'Yes. I'm very sorry, Julian. I won't let the cat in again.'

Everyone seemed to have forgotten I was still in the room.

'You'd better not,' he said in a quieter voice that somehow sounded even more dangerous than the shouting. 'Or you'll be out on your ear. Plenty of other nurses would jump at a nice little job like this.' He glanced across the room and finally noticed me quivering in the corner by the doors. 'Let that cat out *now* and don't let me ever see it here again.'

Caroline was still crying, and I could tell Laura was shaking as she opened the door for me. But I'm afraid I was too terrified for my own life to stop and give either of them a purr or a tail-wave in goodbye. I shot straight out of the door and round the other side of the house. I wasn't even going to risk running back down the driveway until I was sure that angry man was nowhere around – I'd feel too exposed out in the open. There was a wooden shed just round the corner of the building that gave me a vague memory of the place I was born in. The door was ajar, so I crept inside, found a dark little spot behind some flower pots, and lay there panting and mewing softly to myself, waiting for my heartbeat to settle back down.

You'll find, as you get older, little Charlie, that stress does funny things to us cats. Once I'd calmed down a bit and felt relatively safe, I must have gone straight off to sleep.

The next thing I was aware of was a man's voice. I stiffened, immediately scared again, but soon realised this was a different man, a younger one with a quieter voice.

'So he didn't actually throw the poor little cat out of the door?' he was saying.

'No. But he grabbed him round the neck.' I sat up in surprise. It was Laura, the nurse. I could see her in the doorway of the shed, but I could only see the back view of the young man. 'And when the cat dug his claws in – you couldn't blame him! – Julian dropped him. He wasn't hurt, but it must have really scared him.' I heard her sigh. 'And it was all my fault.'

'Oh, don't say that. You were only trying to do your best for the child, weren't you?'

'Of course I was. The cat was giving her so much pleasure. If only Julian would relent and let her have some company – other than me, I mean. She needs other youngsters to chat to.'

'She doesn't know any kids round here, though, does she? I mean, she hasn't been to school since they moved here. She was in hospital, and since she came out, she's been . . .'

'Lying on the sofa, poor little love. No, I thought it'd be good for her to meet some of the children in the village. But when I suggested that to Julian, it was almost as bad as when he found the cat. Anyone would think all the kids in Little Broomford are carriers of some deadly disease.'

'He's being unreasonable, if you ask me.'

There was a silence for a moment.

'Well,' Laura said, 'I know that's how it seems. And he did really upset me – and Caroline – about the cat. But you know, it's only because he's been so frightened of losing her. He told me, when he first took me on, that since his wife died, Caroline is all he's got, and the shock of her cancer nearly killed him. I know he seems like a bully sometimes but the poor man's been through a lot.'

'That's no excuse,' the man said. 'And as for threatening you with the sack – he's an idiot. He'd be lost without you caring for his daughter. Six days a week, while he works in London. Not many people would do it. He should be grateful you haven't walked out on him.'

'I wouldn't do that,' she replied quietly. 'I care too much about Caroline. And he pays me well. I shouldn't have gone behind his back with the cat. But he won't really get rid of me, you know. It was just bluster.'

'I certainly hope he won't, Laura. Well, I'd better get on with mending that fence over the other side of the paddock. Was there anything you wanted or did you just come out for a chat?'

'Oh, I just came to look for a box of old jigsaw puzzles Caroline's asking for. She thought her dad might have put them in here when they moved in, and forgotten them.'

'I haven't seen anything like that,' he said, turning round and scratching his head. 'But you're welcome to have a look through those boxes at the back.'

'OK, Harry. Thanks. See you later.'

He went off, whistling, and Laura came into the shed and started lifting lids off boxes. I hopped out from behind the flowerpots and meowed a hello at her.

'Oh – Oliver!' she said. 'You made me jump! What are you doing still hanging around here? I'd have thought you'd have run a mile, after our telling-off.'

I probably should have done, too. The last thing I wanted was for that Julian to come out and find me here. Now I'd slept off the stress, I needed to get going. I walked round Laura's legs a couple of times to say goodbye, and to my surprise she sat down suddenly on one of the boxes and picked me up, holding me close to her.

'What am I going to do, Oliver?' she said softly against my fur. 'I must be crazy to care about him like I do. He can be so mean sometimes, but I know that's not the real Julian. He's just beside himself with worry all the time about Caroline. I wish I could tell him how I feel. All I want is to be able to look after him and make him happy again. But he's not interested in me, or anyone else, apart from his daughter.'

To be honest I couldn't quite believe what I was hearing. I know humans can be quite peculiar in the way they choose their mates, but surely this nice female could find someone kinder and gentler than that bad-tempered cat-hating Julian? I felt quite sorry for her, though – she must have had some kind of problem in her head. He'd been really nasty to her and she was still making excuses for him. Sometimes, Charlie, I wonder if I'll ever understand humans at all.

CHAPTER
SEVENTEEN

As I finally made my way home from the Big House, I bumped into Suki. She was looking as cross as Tabby had done when I saw him the previous week.

'Oh, hello,' I said. 'I . . . er . . . understand congratulations are in order.'

'No, they're not,' she said very sharply. 'Think about it, Ollie. How would *you* feel if your tummy was going to swell up until you could hardly move, and then you were going to go through hours of agony and end up with a mob of squealing kittens to feed?'

'Well, put like that . . .' I said, feeling awkward. 'Er, where's Tabby, anyway?'

'That's a very good question.' She flicked her tail at me. 'If you see him, tell him I'm looking for him, would you?'

'OK.' I didn't know which of them to feel the most sympathy for. It does seem unfair that females have to go through all that stuff, but there you go – that's life – and there wasn't really any point her taking it out on Tabby. I was just glad I wasn't a female. If I was, nothing would have persuaded me to mate with a horrible randy male like Tabby.

I looked in all the obvious places for Tabby – round the back of the shop, by the swings on the village green, even at his own house. I went as far as jumping over his garden fence and putting my nose up against his cat flap, but there was no sign of him. He was certainly doing a good job of making himself scarce. In the end I finally tracked him down to the side of the big noisy road at the other end of the village.

'What on earth are you doing here?' I shouted at him. I had to shout, because of the noise of the cars racing past.

'Thinking about running across to the other side,' he said morosely.

'Don't be ridiculous! The cars will trample you as soon as you set paw on the road.'

'Maybe. But if they don't, I can escape.'

'Oh yes? Escape where, exactly?' I was getting cross with him now. 'Do you have any idea how it feels to be lost, with no home to go to, and nothing to eat or drink? Have you ever been cornered by a fox, or left in a sack to die? No, of course you haven't, you've had a lovely home with nice humans to feed you and pamper you the whole of your life. How can you even *talk* about escaping?'

He hung his head. 'Sorry, Ollie,' he said. 'I know, you're right. I've been a lucky cat all my life, and I haven't had to go through anything scary like you have. And I'm sorry I've been rude to you lately, as well. You've been a good friend to me. I don't deserve you.'

'Oh, don't start getting all melodramatic on me,' I said impatiently. 'Just get away from this horrible road before we both end up getting hurt. Come on.'

He followed me back up the hill, and when we got to the village green we sat under one of the benches and washed each other's faces like we were brothers.

'Is it just because of Suki?' I asked him eventually. 'Is she still yowling at you? I bumped into her a bit earlier and I must say she seemed . . . um . . . keen to see you.'

'Just wants to have another go at me, I suppose. I preferred her before she found out she was expecting. She was nice then – gentle, and sexy. Now, whenever we see each other it almost turns into a cat fight. At the end of the day, she was just as keen about the mating as I was.'

'Well look,' I said, 'maybe you should just let her blame you, if it makes her feel better. After all, it *is* her who has to get a fat tummy, and go through agony to produce the kittens.' I was just repeating what Suki had said, of course. I had no idea how these things actually worked. 'You might even *like* the kittens when they're born.'

'Huh. I doubt it. But you're probably right. Maybe I'll go and see her tomorrow. Will you come with me?'

'Oh. I don't think that's a good idea, Tabs.'

'*Please*, Ollie. You're so much better than me at under-standing how females think.'

'Yeah, well, that's because of being neutered, I suppose.'

'I'm beginning to envy you. Seriously, at least you have your freedom, and don't feel like you're going to spend the rest of your life being shouted at by a vindictive female who didn't want to have kittens.'

I laughed. 'You'd better try and persuade your owners to take you to the vet, then. Come on, let's walk home together. I'm getting hungry. And I want to tell you what happened to *me* today. You think you have a stressful life? You've got no idea.'

*

As we walked, I told him about the Big House, and Caroline, and being caught by her father.

'*What?*' he kept saying. And, 'I *told* you not to go back there!'

'I know you did,' I agreed. 'And I probably should have listened to you, but I felt like that poor little girl needed me.'

'Your trouble is, you're too soft-hearted, Ollie. And you didn't believe me when I told you there was an angry man there, did you?'

'No. I think he's only there sometimes at weekends, though. So what I'm thinking is, I might go back on Monday.'

'*What!*' he yelled at me again. 'Are you completely raving mad? You've just told me how terrified you were, how he picked you up and dropped you.'

'Only because I dug my claws in.'

'But now you're defending him.'

'No, I'm not, at all. Although it's funny, he was just as horrible to the Laura female as he was to me. But *she* defended him. She actually really likes him. She told me, when she found me in the shed.'

'Yes, but there's no accounting for humans' stupidity, as you well know. We cats have more sense. If you go back there, I'll . . . I'll wash my paws of you!'

We'd reached my foster homes now. I stopped outside the gate to Daniel and Nicky's cottage and turned to face Tabby.

'Did I, or did I not, save your life today?' I asked him straight. 'Didn't I stop you from running out onto the bypass?'

'Not exactly. I probably wouldn't have done it. But thanks anyway,' he added quickly.

'Well, at least I hope I've talked some sense into you. And have I, or have I not, agreed to come with you to talk to Suki tomorrow, even though I really don't think I ought to be getting involved?'

'Yes, and I'm grateful. I appreciate it.'

'So I'm going to ask you to do something for me, in return. To show how much you appreciate it.'

'Go on. What?'

'Come with me on Monday, to the Big House.'

He jumped back as if I'd shot him.

'Not on your life! Sorry, Ollie, but no way. What do you take me for?'

'What do I take you for? A good friend, I hope. And anyway, you're always fond of saying that I'm a timid little thing. Well, if that's the case, and if you're so much bigger and tougher than me, what are you so scared of?'

'I'm not *scared*,' he retorted, puffing out his chest. 'I just don't see the point of it.'

'The point is, that little girl's been very ill and Laura said that ever since I've been visiting her, she's been getting better. So if I *stop* visiting her, she's going to get worse again, isn't she?'

Tabby looked a bit uncomfortable. 'You don't know that for sure.'

'But I wouldn't want it on my conscience. And if you don't come with me, to protect me, because you're so much bigger and braver than me' – I put a lot of emphasis on the *bigger* and *braver* – 'it'll be on your conscience too, Tabs.'

'Oh, now, hang on a minute!'

'And you don't really want anything *else* on your conscience, do you, what with Suki and her kittens?'

'I thought you were on my side.'

'I am, I am. But I'm just saying . . . look, I've made my mind up. Although it's true, I *was* terrified today, and I am only *little* and *timid*, I'm going back on Monday, even if it's just to make sure Caroline's all right. And if *I'm* willing to risk it, but you won't come with me, well, what does that make you?'

'A cat with a bit more common sense?'

'No. A scaredy-cat.'

It was a terrible insult. I waited for him to clout me with one of his big paws. But instead, he looked down at the pavement, and swished his tail a couple of times. And then he looked back at me and raised a paw in surrender.

'OK, I give in. If you're determined to go, I'd better come with you, or it'll be *you* I have on my conscience when the angry man gets you.'

'He won't be there, I'm telling you. We'll go in the morning. I heard them say he goes to the place they call London.'

'All right. But don't forget I'm counting on you tomorrow, then, to come and see Suki with me.'

'Of course. Call for me here after breakfast, all right?'

We meowed our farewells, and I went in to see how Nicky and Daniel were. My head was aching at the thought of all these problems I was trying to sort out. It had been a traumatic day, and it had taken all my powers of persuasion to talk that rascal Tabby round. I must admit I was feeling pretty pleased with myself for the way I'd managed it. But most of all, I just wanted a nice bowl of Kitty-Chunks and a long, long nap.

I slept for a long time, in a comfy chair in Nicky and Daniel's sitting room, and when I woke up it was getting dark and I could hear Nicky saying, in a loud voice out in the hallway:

'*There* you are! For God's sake, Dan, I was just about to send out the search parties. What the hell took you so long?'

'Sorry, Nick. I got waylaid.' He didn't *sound* sorry. He actually sounded quite pleased with himself.

'You did get some firewood, I hope?'

'Yes, look. A whole bag full. And then, when I was on my way back, the guy who lives in the corner house was trying to start his car.'

'Right. Very interesting.' It's funny, with humans, Charlie. They so often seem to mean the opposite of what they say. Nicky didn't sound the least bit interested, in fact she went on quite impatiently, 'Now, it's freezing in this house and you must be cold too, being out all that time. If I make you a hot cup of tea, do you think you could use some of that wood to get the fire going? Or is it too damp?'

'It might be. But I'll give it a try.'

He came into the lounge, shrugging off his jacket and putting his rucksack down next to the fireplace.

'Oh, hello, Ollie,' he said as I stood up in the chair and did some stretching and yawning. 'Have you been asleep in here? Had a busy day?'

'You don't know the half of it,' I meowed.

I watched him for a while as he built up the wood in the fireplace. Nicky was quite right, it was really cold in the room. If it was going to take a while for that fire to warm us up, I'd be better off going next door and getting into my hammock on the radiator. But just as I was about to ask Daniel to let me out, Nicky came back into the room with two mugs of steaming tea on a tray.

'Sorry I snapped,' she said, putting the tray down on the little table. 'I just couldn't understand why you were taking so long. And I was getting cold. I nearly put the heating on.'

He stood up and pulled her into his arms. 'You should have done. You must look after yourself, Nick. I don't want you catching a chill and getting ill. Not now.'

'Oh, don't worry,' she said. 'The baby's plenty warm enough in here.' She patted her tummy. 'Anyway, what *were* you doing all that time?'

'I tried to tell you. The guy on the corner – his name's Tony . . .'

'Couldn't start his car. So you spent half an hour or more watching him?'

'No! It was obvious what the problem was – his battery was flat. I knocked on the car window and asked if he wanted some help.'

'Ah!' She laughed. 'I might have guessed.'

'Well, I couldn't just watch him going on and on turning the ignition and risking flooding his engine, could I. He and his wife were supposed to be going to visit their daughter. They're pensioners, and I'm not being funny but he seemed a bit clueless about cars. I asked him if he had a battery charger, and he looked at me like I was talking Swahili! His wife told him to take me round to his garage to have a look for myself. *He doesn't know what he's got in there,* she told me. And yes, there was a battery charger, still in its box like it had never been used, so . . .'

'You came to the rescue.' Nicky laughed. 'Well, that was nice of you.'

'The battery's still on charge, of course. I'll pop back later and see if I can get it going for him. He phoned his daughter to say they'd go tomorrow instead. I told him he really needs a new battery. But at least he should be OK temporarily, as long as he doesn't leave his lights on or anything silly like that.'

'You sound really . . . kind of fired-up.' Nicky looked at him a bit sadly. 'I'd almost forgotten how much you always enjoyed it – tinkering around with cars.'

'Hardly tinkering around. Just putting a battery on charge. Not like getting down and dirty taking an engine out.' He shrugged and picked up his mug to take a sip of tea. 'Never mind. One of these days perhaps I'll at least have time to start playing around with our *own* old wreck. That'd be a start. As things are, it's a good job we only use it to drive to the station and back. It's amazing it even got through its MOT. If it was a horse, they'd have put it down.'

Nicky laughed. 'You *will* get time, Dan, when the spring comes, and the lighter evenings. If you can do it up a bit, we should probably sell it. We can hardly afford to fill it up, never mind paying the tax and insurance. We were mad to buy it in the first place, even though it *was* cheap. We'd be better off using the bus.'

'Just another of our crap decisions,' he agreed, sighing.

And they both stood there, sipping their tea, watching the wood begin to glow orange and red in the fireplace, and I decided it was time to meow my urgent need to be let out.

By the time I jumped through the cat flap in Sarah and Martin's kitchen, I was hungry again, despite having had some food earlier next door. Nobody seemed to be around downstairs, but I could hear voices from the bathroom. I padded upstairs, enjoying the warmth of the central heating. The bathroom door was half open and there was a steamy, soapy feel in the air. I could tell from this, and from the splashes and laughter coming from the room, that the children were in the bath. I've never understood why humans seem to find sitting in water so enjoyable, but I certainly wasn't going to get near enough to get splashed myself. I darted into the girls' bedroom and waited on Rose's bed for someone to notice me and remember to feed me.

After a while I heard Martin calling from downstairs.

'Hello! I've finished in the shed now.' Presumably doing his *Saturday pottering* again. 'Shall I start putting some dinner on?'

'Yes please!' I meowed loudly.

'Oh – Ollie's back,' I heard Grace saying in the bathroom. 'I can hear him in our bedroom, Mummy.'

'He must be hungry. He's been out all day, hasn't he,' Sarah said. 'Martin, will you put some food down for Ollie, please? I'm just chasing the kids out of the bath, then we'll all be down. I've told them they can stay up and watch TV for a while tonight once they're in their pyjamas.'

'Where does Ollie go when he's out all day?' Rose asked. 'I hope he doesn't run into the road,' she added quietly.

'I'm sure he won't,' Sarah said, but they'd all gone quiet and I knew Rose had started thinking about Sooty again.

I jumped off the bed, anticipating my dinner, but just then Grace came bounding into the room with her dressing-gown on.

'Hello, Ollie,' she said, squatting down to stroke me. 'You won't get too close to the roads, will you?'

'No,' I meowed firmly in Cat. 'I'm not an idiot like my friend Tabby.'

She put her lips close to my ear and did this thing humans call whispering. It's like talking, you see, Charlie, but without their voice coming out. It tickled my ear.

'Don't tell anyone,' she said. 'But I'm going to buy Rose a new cat. I mean, one to keep forever, because you're going to go back to your real home one day, aren't you?'

And with that, she ran off downstairs, while I followed more slowly, my heart in my paws. So it was true. They were going to get rid of me. Or even worse, bring a new cat into the house who would resent me, as a lodger, and make my life difficult.

I was so upset I almost didn't enjoy my dinner.

CHAPTER
EIGHTEEN

CHAPTER
EIGHTEEN

The next morning, as promised, I was outside the front gate bright and early, washing the breakfast off my whiskers while I waited for Tabby. He eventually turned up, looking as gloomy as a cat in a cage.

'I wish I didn't have to face her,' he said as we set off to look for Suki. 'She's just going to give me another mouthful of abuse.'

'So let's get it over with. Remember, just try to be sympathetic. I've heard females have something called *hormones* going on when they get pregnant. I don't know what it is, but it probably isn't very nice.'

'All right, Ollie, I'll do my best. But be a good cat and back me up if she starts on me.'

Suki was sitting on a windowsill of her house, staring out. When she saw us coming along the road she sat up straight and fixed us with a really mean, vicious glare.

'This doesn't bode well,' Tabby groaned.

We waited in her front garden as Suki jumped down from the windowsill, her tail already flicking dangerously, and disappeared from view.

'She'll be heading straight for the cat flap,' he said, 'and then straight for my throat.'

'Stay calm. Don't go on the offensive,' I advised him, although I obviously wasn't looking forward to the confrontation either.

'Look what the dog dragged in,' Suki meowed nastily as she reappeared round the side of the house. 'I thought you must have done a runner, Tabby. Haven't seen you around since our last fight. Too scared to face me, were you?'

'No, I just don't want to fight with you,' he said, in a pathetic whining mew. I looked at him in surprise. I'd never heard Tabby sound so unsure of himself before. 'What's done is done, Suki.'

'Yes, but *you're* not the one walking around with kittens in your tummy as a result.'

'Look, I'm sorry, but . . .'

'Don't say *but*,' I said to him very quietly. 'Just *sorry*.'

'Sorry isn't good enough. And who asked you, Oliver?' She immediately turned her venom on me. 'Who asked you to get involved anyway?'

'Tabby did,' I admitted. 'But it's true, he *is* sorry. He was telling me yesterday how sorry he is. He wishes the pair of you didn't mate in the first place, don't you, Tabby?'

'Do I?' Tabby gave me a puzzled look. 'Oh, er . . . I suppose I do, yes, in the circumstances.'

'So now you're saying you didn't even enjoy it?' she shrieked.

'No! No, I'm not saying that.' He got up and turned around a couple of times on the spot, looking even more uncomfortable than I felt, while Suki just sat there, glaring, waiting. 'Look,' he said again finally, with an air of desperation in his meows. 'You're a nice cat, Suki, and we had fun, didn't we?'

'And now I'm having kittens, you're dumping me.'

'No! Did I say that? I've only stayed away from you because you've been in such a foul mood.'

I glared at him. That didn't sound like the best thing to say to her.

'I'm *pregnant*!' she hissed at him. 'Of course I'm in a bad mood.'

'All right. But it won't last forever, will it. And then, afterwards, maybe we can get together and have fun again,' Tabby said, looking suddenly considerably brighter.

'What!' she screeched. 'Are you completely off your head? You needn't think you're going to talk me into it again. Anyway, my humans have always said they were going to get me spayed after I'd had one litter. I just don't think they expected it to happen quite so soon. And nor did I,' she added, giving him another reproachful look.

'It must have been a shock for you,' I said, trying for my most sympathetic mew. 'Have your humans not realised yet that you're expecting?'

'No, but I'm sure they soon will. At the rate I'm putting on weight, I won't get through the cat flap for much longer.'

'You still look good to me, Suki,' Tabby purred.

I stared at him. It was unbelievable. Even now he was trying to come on to her. He couldn't seem to help himself. I was *so* glad I didn't have to live my life at the mercy of these strange urges.

'Anyway,' I said, trying to change the subject, 'we think you'll be an excellent mother, don't we, Tabby?'

'Yes, excellent,' he said without much obvious interest. If cats could shrug, his shoulders would have been up round his ears.

'Do you really think so, Ollie?' she said.

And I suddenly realised she was probably frightened. That was why she was being so aggressive. She was still a young female and probably had no idea how she was going to cope with the birth and raising the kittens.

'Of *course* I mean it,' I said. 'You've got exactly the right temperament. It's as if you were born to be a mother. Isn't it, Tabby?'

'Er, yes. Sure.'

'And you know what? I bet once they're born, you're actually going to *love* those kittens,' I went on. 'Little kittens are so cute, everybody loves them – but their mothers always love them best of all.'

Suki was looking at me very strangely.

'That's a nice thing to say, Ollie. But what's the matter? You look like you're going to cry.'

'I'm all right,' I said, turning away. I went and sat a little way away from them, washing myself, trying not to show how much I *did* feel like crying.

'He was taken away from his mother,' I heard Tabby telling Suki very quietly.

'Kittens nearly always leave their mothers,' she retorted. 'We can't keep them all with us forever.'

'No. But I bet when you were a kitten, you at least stayed with your mum until you were old enough to walk, and see properly, and eat meat. I bet you weren't snatched away from your mum and left to die.'

'Oh.'

I turned back to look at her. She'd gone all soft-looking, like she wanted to cry herself.

'Poor Ollie,' she said gently. 'I didn't know. And you've turned out to be such a nice cat, haven't you, despite everything. Unlike *some* males I could mention!' she added with another venomous glare at Tabby. She stood up and stretched. 'Anyway, I'll be seeing you both, I suppose. I need my rest. I've got my kittens to think about now.'

We watched her turn tail and head back round the side of her house.

'Well,' Tabby said, 'I think I handled that quite well, don't you?

Back at Sarah and Martin's house, it was looking very festive. Martin had put twinkly lights over the front door and the windows, and the children were helping Sarah to put decorations up in the lounge. They were singing songs about red nosed reindeers and the three kings of Orient, whoever they were, and talking about making Christmas cards for their school friends. After they'd had their Sunday lunch they all went out to visit some friends in another village. Left on my own, I sat on the back of the sofa, looking at the pretty baubles twinkling on the Christmas tree. A couple of them were within easy reach of my paws from where I was sitting. They were just hanging there, sparkling at me, begging to be swatted. Nobody would ever know, would they? I reached out one paw and batted a big silver one. It swung backwards and forwards prettily on the tree for a minute. Very nice. I batted it a bit harder. Oh, it was *so* satisfying – I could keep this up all day. A little Father Christmas figure was swaying just above my head. I lay on my back and reached up with my back paws, giving it a good kick, then jumped up again and swiped at a red shiny bauble on a higher branch. By now the adrenaline was really pumping. How far up could I reach? With a little jump I could hit that big glittery golden one . . . pow! Oh, drat. I misjudged the jump slightly and instead of landing safely on the back of the sofa, crashed through the lower branches of the tree, ending up tumbling off the bucket and onto the floor. A shower of pine needles fell over me, followed by two or three baubles and some tinsel, which had got itself round my neck. I ran for the kitchen, shaking the tinsel and pine needles off as I went. Phew! That had ended up a bit scary. Just as well nobody was watching. I gave myself a good wash and decided to pop round to see Nicky and Daniel, so that I wouldn't be tempted by any more illicit play with the baubles.

The cottage next door was so bare compared with Sarah and Martin's house. Nicky was cleaning her little kitchen in silence while Daniel was busy putting something he called *draught excluder* around their doors and windows instead of twinkling lights.

'Cheer up, babe,' he said, coming into the kitchen and putting his arms around her waist from behind. 'Things are going to get better.'

'Are they, though, Dan? It's only two and a bit weeks now till my parents are due to come. It's nice that Sarah and Martin are putting them up overnight, but I've still got no idea how we're going to make it seem anything like a proper Christmas.'

'We'll get presents for them, and for your brothers. And I'll get a turkey, and all the trimmings, I promise. I'll put it all on my credit card.'

'Your card's already maxed out. Don't be stupid. We're in enough debt as it is.'

'So a little bit more won't hurt. Come on, Nick, it's nearly Christmas. We need to think positive.'

Just then there was a knock on the door. They looked at each other in surprise.

'Can't imagine who that might be,' Daniel muttered.

He went to open the door, and I heard him say, 'Oh, hello again, Tony. Come in, for God's sake, it's freezing out there. How's the car?' he added as he closed the door and led the way into the kitchen.

'Running perfectly smoothly, thanks to you,' the other man was saying. His voice sounded pleasant enough, but nevertheless he was still a strange male, and my heart was doing its usual little dance of fear. 'I hope I didn't keep your husband too long yesterday,' he added to Nicky.

'Not at all,' she said with a smile. 'He loves nothing better than tinkering with cars, and he doesn't often get the opportunity. I'm Nicky, by the way – I don't think we've met. We only moved here a few months ago.'

'I'm Tony.' He suddenly caught sight of me cowering under the little kitchen table. 'Oh, your cat looks just like the one that used to live in the pub.'

'He is! It's Oliver. He spends some of his time with us, and some with Martin and Sarah next door – since the fire, you know,' Daniel explained. He picked me up and gave me a little stroke. 'He's a bit shy with strangers, but he's a lovely boy, aren't you, Ollie?'

I purred in response, feeling much safer in Daniel's arms.

'I was never a regular in the Forester's, but I thought I recognised him. I heard George had had to relocate temporarily. Good of you and Martin to take care of the cat.'

'Oh, it's been nice to have him around, when we're here, that is. We both work in London all week.'

'Do you? I don't envy you. I used to commute myself, before I retired a couple of years back. Not a lot of fun, is it, and so expensive these days.'

Daniel glanced at Nicky and nodded. 'You're right there.'

'Would you like a cup of tea or something, Tony?' Nicky asked.

'No, thank you, I'm sure you're busy. I just came to thank you again, really, for your help. This is just by way of a small recompense for your time.' He held out a carrier bag, adding, 'It's not much.'

'Oh!' Daniel blinked and went a bit pink. 'There wasn't any need . . .'

There was a clinking of bottles as he put me down and took the bag from Tony. I knew that sound quite well, of course, from my days at the pub. Daniel peered inside the bag and exclaimed: 'No, really, you don't have to do this!'

'I insist. It's the least we could do. If you hadn't helped me out I'd have had to call someone from the garage in town, and you can imagine what they'd have charged me, just for my own stupidity in letting the battery go flat. It's only a couple of bottles of plonk.'

'And this too?' Daniel asked, lifting something else out of the bag. It was a bowl of some sort, covered with that plastic stuff they call cling film.

'Just a Christmas pudding,' Tony said with a short laugh. 'Chuck it out if you don't want it.'

'Of course we wouldn't chuck it out,' Nicky said, looking shocked. 'But surely you want it yourselves for Christmas?'

'My wife makes half a dozen of the things every year, love, and there's only us, and my daughter and son-in-law. I think she wants to feed the entire village. She always gives one to the WI for a raffle prize, and one to the Scouts' bazaar – not that they're having one of course, this year, because of the hall.' He shrugged. 'If it's any good to you, please take it and enjoy it. They're good, I have to say, her puddings. There's just too many of them.'

And, laughing again, he turned to leave. 'Hope to see you both again before Christmas, anyway. Thanks again, Daniel.'

'No, thank *you*, for these,' Daniel said, still staring into the bag.

'How kind of him!' Nicky exclaimed after she'd seen him out. 'Can you believe what he said? *Just a couple of bottles of plonk*? They look like good wines, Dan. We'll have to put them away for Christmas Day.'

'Yes, I suppose we should,' he said, looking regretful.

She laughed. 'And *chuck the pudding away if you don't want it*! As if! How lovely – at least we'll have *that* to serve up to my family now. I could even pretend to Mum that I made it myself.'

Daniel put both arms round her then and they clung together, laughing. It was so nice to see them happy for once. I purred my delight at them, walking round their legs, and it felt like we were all doing a little dance together. For a minute or two, you know, it actually felt warmer in that chilly little kitchen.

I didn't get a particularly warm welcome, though, when I went back to Sarah and Martin's house. Sarah had the hoover out – I always hated the noise it made, so I tried to run straight upstairs. But she saw me, turned off the hoover and called out to me in quite a stern voice:

'Yes, you might well run away, Oliver! Look at the mess I'm having to clear up in here. Three baubles broken, pine needles everywhere, tinsel strewn through the lounge . . .'

'Sorry!' I squawked in Cat as I scarpered up the stairs. 'I got carried away.'

I was worried she might be so cross with me that she'd go and get the new cat straight away and send me packing.

I slunk into the girls' bedroom to hide under one of their duvets.

'Cats!' I heard Sarah exclaim out loud to herself. 'Almost as much trouble as kids.'

I couldn't quite work out whether that was good or bad. But just before the hoover started its noise again, I was surprised to hear her laughing to herself.

Phew! Perhaps she still loved me after all.

CHAPTER
NINETEEN

Tabby and I had another early start the following day, and again I wasn't looking forward to it. However strongly I'd insisted on Tabby coming with me back to the Big House, I didn't really feel brave about it at all.

What's that, Charlie? You think I *must* have been a brave cat to go back after what happened? Well, it's nice of you to say so, little one. But honestly, my paws were shaking as I went to call for Tabby on the way there.

'Morning!' I said as he came out of his cat flap, looking like he'd just woken up. 'Blimey. Didn't you get much sleep last night? Your fur's all over the place.'

'Had a bit of a late one out on the tiles,' he admitted, yawning. 'There's a new little Burmese moved in just down the road here. Cute as anything – slim little paws, beautiful green eyes . . .'

'Tabby!' I was so taken aback, I almost forgot how nervous I was about our destination. 'You're still going through all this trauma with Suki about giving her kittens! How can you . . .'

'Oh, I think Suki will come round, you know, after the chat we had yesterday,' he said breezily. 'And meanwhile, there's no point letting the grass grow under your paws, Ollie.'

I had to laugh. 'You're incorrigible,' I said. 'But I can forgive you anything, as long as you're still up for coming with me this morning.'

'I'm not up for it at all, actually. I think you're a nutcase. But you're right, I can't let a little fella like you go into danger on your own, without the protection of someone bigger and braver and more macho like me.'

'Oh, give it a rest,' I said, nudging him with my head in a friendly way. 'Let's get going.'

As we walked up the hill together I started telling Tabby my worries about Sarah and Martin getting a new cat.

'So what?' he said. 'You're not living with them forever, are you? And not *just* them, anyway – I thought you said you live in the house next door too? All right for some, having two homes to choose from.'

'I know it sounds nice, and yes, I am lucky. But I'd rather be back with George than with either of them. That's not going to happen for ages, though. They haven't even started rebuilding the pub yet, have they? And if Sarah and Martin don't want me anymore, I'll have to live with Nicky and Daniel permanently.'

'Don't you like them?'

'Yes, of course I do. But they're both out all day, working, and the house is really cold, and they're not usually very happy because of the money thing humans worry about all the time. I'd feel ever so lonely if I couldn't go to Sarah and Martin's house too.'

'I see. But why do you think they'll chuck you out, even if they do get a new cat?'

'I've been a kind of replacement for their old one who got run over.'

'Oh yes, poor old Sooty.' Tabby nodded at me. 'That was horrible, poor chap.'

'I never met him.'

'He was quite old, didn't go out a lot. I reckon that was why the car got him – he couldn't run away fast enough. Shame about the little human, too – broke her paw, didn't she?'

'Yes. She's sweet. They say I've cheered her up. But if she gets a permanent new cat, that's obviously going to be much better for her, isn't it.' I sighed. 'And the new cat won't want me around.'

'It might do. After all, Ollie, you wouldn't pose too much of a threat to another male.'

'Well *thanks*!'

'Don't mention it. And on the other hand, it might be a female.' He nudged me and gave a little suggestive mew of laughter. 'But of course,' he added, 'that'd be wasted on you, wouldn't it.'

'You've got a one-track mind, Tabby,' I complained. 'I wish your humans *would* get you neutered. We might be able to have a serious conversation then, without the subject of females coming up every five minutes.'

We'd reached the gates of the Big House by now, and we both fell silent as we squeezed through the iron pattern and into the grounds.

'Don't be frightened, Ollie,' Tabby said eventually as we walked stealthily down the drive – but I noticed his voice was shaking. 'I'll be right behind you.'

I'd have preferred him in front of me, as he was bigger, but there you go.

'This is the room where the little sick human usually is,' I told him quietly when we reached the glass doors. 'We can see her if we look through here.'

'There's nobody in there,' said Tabby, peering over my shoulder into the room.

'No.' How disappointing. 'Perhaps she's still in bed. We *are* quite early, I suppose.'

It's hard to tell, in winter, you see, Charlie. It often still looks like the middle of the night in the morning, and then it looks like the middle of the night again halfway through the afternoon. And then, in the summer, you'll find it's just as tricky because night time doesn't seem to come round all that often at all. We never know where we are – it's quite tiring trying to fathom it out, which is why I find it best to simply sleep as much as possible, regardless.

'So shall we just go home?' Tabby said hopefully.

'No. Not yet. Let's have a quick check around the house. We might see her inside one of the other rooms.'

'You're one crazy cat,' he muttered. 'Lead on, then, if you know the way.'

I led him round the corner and past the steps where I'd jumped up on the windowsill that day to look at the huge empty room. There was no way Caroline would be in *there*.

'I suppose she'll be somewhere upstairs, if she's still asleep in her bedroom,' I said.

I gazed up at the great walls and high roof of the huge house. No chance. Even Tabby wouldn't try to serenade anyone on *that* rooftop. And then I saw it – a little bit further, round a corner of the house and sticking out into the grounds, was one of those glass rooms humans call conservatories.

'Let's just have a quick look in there,' I suggested, and I started to sneak forward along the wall of the house before Tabby could dissuade me. The bottom part of the conservatory was a low brick wall. I waited behind this for Tabby to catch up and then hopped up onto the window ledge and peered through the glass.

It was a cold, frosty morning again, but very sunny, and all the morning sunshine was on this side of the house, so I thought it was quite likely Laura and Caroline might be in here. What I definitely *hadn't* expected was to see Caroline's father instead. I nearly fell off the ledge with fright. What was he doing here? He was supposed to go to the London place today. Had I got the days wrong? He was standing with his back to me, holding his chin in his hand, staring out of one of the windows on the opposite side of the room – thank goodness!

'Is she in there? Can you see her?' Tabby hissed at me from the safety of the ground.

'Ssh!' I warned him.

The window ledge was narrow and I was having trouble keeping my balance. I was just about to jump back down and start running, when I heard a noise from inside. I pricked up my ears. It was him, the father, talking to himself. At first I couldn't quite believe it. But a couple of the windows were a fraction open on my side of the conservatory, despite the cold – perhaps, with all that glass, the sun had made it warm inside – and with my excellent

219

hearing, I was picking up every word. I was so surprised, I forgot to run away and stayed where I was, listening.

'What an idiot,' he was saying. 'What a bloody stupid idiot. What's the matter with me? There was no need to talk to her like that. Threatening to sack her! It'll be my own stupid fault if she walks out now.'

Yes, it will, I thought crossly. *And there was no need to be so horrible to me, either!*

'What's going on?' Tabby called up. 'Are you all right up there?'

'Ssh!' I hissed again. 'I'm listening. Be quiet!'

The man was sighing to himself. I could see his chest and shoulders going up and down.

'I suppose it's too late to apologise. She must already think I'm just an arrogant bully, and now I've made things even worse. I don't know why I behave like this – taking out all my frustration on her. And she's so good with Caroline – so kind, so patient. Not just with Caroline – with me too. Oh, God, what's *wrong* with me? She's the first woman I've felt like this about since you died, Susan—'

Susan? Who was this Susan, and how did she come into it? I put my ear closer to the glass.

'—and there's absolutely no chance she'll forgive me this time. She must hate me, and I don't blame her.' He sighed again. 'What should I do, Sue? Try to talk to her? Maybe just write her a note. That'd be better, wouldn't it – a little note to say I'm sorry. At least then we could put that episode on Saturday behind us and I'll try *again* to be better tempered.'

He was searching in a drawer now, and then, having found a pen and a pad of paper, to my horror he turned round and walked towards my side of the conservatory. Once again I nearly fell off the ledge on top of Tabby, but luckily, the man was looking down at the floor, and just sat down on a chair with his back against my window. His head was so close to mine, if I'd knocked against the glass with my collar he'd have jumped. I knew I was asking for trouble now. I should just go, and be grateful he hadn't seen me. But he was still talking to himself, and if curiosity really did kill the cat, I was probably about to lose a life.

'Dear Laura,' he said out loud as he wrote quickly on his pad. 'The way I spoke to you on Saturday was unforgiveable, so I won't attempt to excuse it. You're so understanding and sympathetic, I don't have to tell you that it's my overwhelming anxiety about Caroline, and the sleepless nights I have, worrying about her condition, that have made me so constantly on edge that I snap at the slightest thing. But there's no excuse for taking it out on you, so I can only appeal to your kind and caring nature, to overlook my bad temper once again and accept my apology. If you only knew how much I actually care about you . . .'

He stopped, chewing his pen, staring out of the opposite window again. Then he suddenly got up, almost scaring me, yet again, into toppling off the ledge, and he ripped the page out of the pad. He screwed it up fiercely into a ball and lobbed it into a wastepaper basket.

'What's the point?' he exclaimed crossly to himself. 'She hates me and I deserve it. I'm wasting my time.' He glanced at his watch. 'Oh, God – what am I doing still here? I've missed my train now. Where are my car keys? There's probably no parking left at the station. Damn! I'm going to have to drive into the city, now.'

And with that he strode out of the room, and I threw myself off the window ledge.

'Quick!' I hissed at Tabby. 'Hide!'

We belted across the grass and ducked behind a shrub. A few minutes later the door of a garage block on the corner opened and a big, sleek, shiny car purred out and disappeared round the side of the house.

'He's gone,' I said with relief. 'We're safe.'

'Was that *him*?' Tabby squeaked. 'He was *here*? Why didn't you say? Why didn't we run off straight away?'

'Because he was talking to himself, and . . .'

'To *himself*? See, I told you he was mad.'

'I wanted to listen. And it was very interesting. Now . . .'

'Now we can go home,' he said, looking all around him nervously. 'I don't like it here.'

'It's fine now he's gone. He'll be at work all day. Come on, I'm going inside.'

'No!' he squawked, running in front of me and trying to block my way. 'Don't be an idiot, Ollie, it isn't safe. Come back!'

'There's a window open up here,' I told him, jumping up onto the ledge again. 'We can easily squeeze through.'

'Speak for yourself,' he muttered, but with a bit of huffing and puffing, he followed me, jumping down after me into the conservatory and still muttering his disapproval. 'What now?' he asked. 'We *are* trespassing, Ollie – I suppose you do realise that? What *are* you doing?'

I'd made a dive for the wastepaper basket and knocked it over.

'Here it is,' I said, picking up the screwed-up page in my teeth. 'Come on! I'm taking this to show Laura.'

'The cat's gone completely bonkers,' he moaned to himself, nevertheless trotting obediently after me. 'We're going to get thrown out, probably *kicked* out . . .'

Just then a shadow fell over us. I glanced up, and to my relief, it was only Laura. But she didn't look pleased. I suppose she didn't want any more trouble for allowing one cat into the house, never mind two.

'What . . .?' she started. I dropped the ball of paper near her feet, but she didn't even notice, kicking it with one foot as she came towards me. 'Oliver! How did you get in, and who is *this*?' She gave Tabby a disapproving look, and he shrank away from her. The paper ball had rolled towards him, and he promptly knocked it back to me, trying to show it had nothing to do with him.

'Oh, *look*,' came a little voice from behind Laura. It was Caroline, holding onto Laura's arm as she watched us. 'Ollie's brought a friend with him, and they're *playing*!' She laughed. 'Aren't they cute?'

'*Cute*!' Tabby meowed to me indignantly.

'Yes!' I replied. 'Be cute. Play!'

I knocked the ball of paper to him with my paw, and waited for him to bat it across to me again. I knew he wouldn't be able to resist the ball-of-paper game, however nervous he was feeling. When he knocked it back to me, I deliberately sent it towards Laura's feet.

'They want us to play with them,' Caroline squealed.

But this time Laura bent down and picked up the paper. I held my breath. Was she just going to throw it back in the bin? No! She smoothed it out and started reading it. I watched her face. Her eyes widened, and when she got to the end, she flushed very red. For a moment, we were all frozen there – Laura staring at the note, Tabby and I poised to make a run for it, Caroline watching us.

'Huh!' Laura exclaimed suddenly, making me jump. 'Why am I bothering to even *read* this nonsense? He must have been drunk when he wrote it.'

'What is it?' Caroline asked.

'Just a bit of rubbish.' And she screwed it back up and dropped it in the bin. 'And I'm sorry, Caroline, but the cats have to go. You know what your father said.'

She opened the conservatory door and shooed us out.

Well, at least, I suppose, we didn't have to climb back out of the window.

CHAPTER
TWENTY

So I'd been through all that trauma, and achieved precisely nothing. I felt a failure. I'd tried to be a helpful cat, a cat who made people happy, and in the end all I'd been was a silly little cat who got people into trouble.

'Don't be too hard on yourself,' Tabby said cheerfully. Funny how he'd perked up now we were on the way home and out of danger – but then, to be fair, at least he did come with me and didn't run away when the heat was on, like a scaredy-cat. 'It was an adventure. Something we can show off to the females about.'

I laughed and rubbed heads with him. 'Thanks, Tabs. I'm glad we're friends.'

'Me too. You're a much braver little cat than I ever thought. I don't know why you used to let me call you timid.'

But in my little heart, I felt sad and sorry. I'd started off my new life as a foster cat with too high an opinion of myself, I now realised. Because I'd given a few people in the village the idea of getting together in their homes, I'd thought I was the mouse's whiskers, but I obviously wasn't as clever as I thought I was. I went back through the cat flap into Sarah's kitchen and spent most of the day asleep.

When the children came home from school, the rest of the Foxes came round, and spent some time playing with me while Sarah looked through the papers they'd been writing about me during the last few weeks.

'Well done, girls,' she said eventually. 'You've all completed your "Pet" projects now and they're very good. I'll pass these on to Brown Owl, and you can get started on the other sections of the badge.'

The children clamoured around her as she read out some options from a book.

'The zoo!' Grace shouted. 'Yes! Let's go to the zoo!'

'Yes, the zoo!' they all chorused.

Sarah laughed. 'All right, I'll talk to Brown Owl about it, and perhaps we can take you together. We could go on the train, during the Christmas holiday.'

'Bye, Ollie,' the girls called out as they trooped off to their homes.

I slunk back out to the kitchen and lay down in my basket, curling up with my tail over my head. Even the Foxes didn't need me anymore. Pretty soon the family were going to replace me with another cat, and then there'd be nobody left who cared about me. Oh, if only that fire had never happened. If only I were still in the pub with George. I mewed myself quietly back to sleep.

I didn't really cheer up until the following evening, when Sarah was rushing around the house excitedly, moving extra chairs into the lounge and tidying up, because it was her turn to have the WI ladies there.

'Nicky next door is going to come tonight,' she told Martin, who had put on his old coat and was going out to the shed, with a mug of beer in his hand, to *make himself scarce*. 'I'm really glad I've persuaded her. It will do her good to meet some of the other women.'

I was glad too, and I felt sorry then for thinking I'd have nobody else in the world if Sarah and Martin didn't want me. Although their cottage was cold, Nicky and Daniel were lovely humans and I know they liked me too. If it hadn't been for Daniel, I might still be up that tree in the wood, or in the fox's tummy, I reminded myself sternly with a little shudder.

When all the females started arriving, I sat in my hammock on the radiator so that I could listen to them chat. To my surprise, they started off by standing up in a row and singing a song about some place called Jerusalem. Some of them had loud screechy voices and I thought I'd better join in, to try to keep them in tune. I lifted my head and yowled as loudly as I could. They all started smiling and as soon as the song was finished there was a loud burst of laughter from everyone and they turned to me and clapped their paws. Believe me, Charlie, you'll find female humans can be even stranger than the males at times.

After that, they all sat down, apart from one, who stood at the front reading things out to them about money they needed to pay and trips they might be going on.

'And as we all know, ladies,' she went on, 'the Christmas party is cancelled this year but Sarah has kindly offered to have us all back here on the Saturday after Christmas, for a buffet lunch. Some of you have offered to bring cakes or sandwiches – you know who you are – and please all bring your own drinks, or all you'll get is a glass of water.'

They all laughed again. They seemed a cheerful bunch. Nicky was sitting next to Sarah, smiling and appearing to enjoy herself.

'Finally, I have a plea for help from Louise.' The female in charge nodded at her. 'If anyone knows of a qualified child minder who could work part-time, please let her know. She's absolutely desperate for someone to look after Freya and Henry after Kay finishes. She's had no luck with adverts in the paper . . .'

'There's a notice about swapping kids on different days, on the board,' someone at the back of the room called out.

'I know.' Louise turned to face her. 'But it's no good for me. I work five mornings a week. I'm on the waiting lists of two nurseries in Great Broomford, but it could take ages to get a place.'

There was a murmur of sympathy around the room.

'I could help you out for the odd morning, love,' one of the older women said. 'Not that I'm qualified or anything, but I've brought up my own kids and helped with the grandkids.'

'Well, me too,' said Sarah. 'I only work part-time from home, so I could help out sometimes.'

A couple of others joined in, offering help on odd mornings here and there.

'That's really kind of you all,' Louise said, 'but I really need definite, reliable cover for the whole week. My mum might come and stay for a few weeks, but I can't expect . . .'

She tailed off, shaking her head. 'I'm going to lose my job if I can't sort something out.'

I saw Sarah glance at Nicky, who was looking at the floor. Later, after one of the other women had stood up and talked to them all for a long time about her trip to Peru and shown them her photos, and they were all milling around chatting to each other, I followed Nicky out to the kitchen where she'd gone to help Sarah make tea and coffee.

'You should talk to Louise, you know,' Sarah said.

'What's the point? Daniel told me he saw her advert on the notice board. She only wants someone for twenty hours a week, and she won't be able to pay me what I need.'

'But Nicky, you won't want to work more than twenty hours, once your own baby's arrived. Trust me, you'll probably even struggle with that. I know – I *know* you need the money, but perhaps, if things are that bad and Daniel isn't earning enough, you'll need to think about claiming some benefits. I'm sorry to be so personal,' she added more quietly, 'it's only because I'm concerned about you.'

'If my parents thought we were on benefits,' Nicky said in a tight voice like she was being strangled, 'they'd go mad. They'd say we were letting them down, and they'd blame Daniel.'

'Or perhaps they'd help you out a bit,' Sarah retorted.

'No. They'd rather I left him and went back home to them.'

They poured tea in silence for a minute, then Nicky started carrying cups into the lounge.

'You've upset her now,' I meowed at Sarah.

'Oh, Ollie.' She looked down at me, shaking her head. 'I shouldn't have said anything, should I? But I just want to help her. What shall I do?'

'Don't ask me,' I said, rubbing against her leg in sympathy, 'I make a mess of everything.'

'It's no good.' She picked up the last two cups, ready to go back to the lounge. 'I'm going to have a quiet word with Louise myself. Call me interfering, but if I don't say anything I might always regret it.'

Perhaps she was a bit like me – trying her best to help people, but not always succeeding.

I don't think Nicky noticed Sarah and Louise chatting quietly in the corner, or Louise glancing in Nicky's direction with interest – because by then she was talking to someone else herself. I was eavesdropping as usual, of course, and I'd gathered from the conversation that this was the wife of Tony, who'd had the sick car, and her name was Cath.

'I'm *so* glad I've met you, dear,' she said, beaming at Nicky. 'You have no idea how grateful Tony and I were to your husband for charging the battery up for us. We are both so useless with car problems.'

'He was just glad to help, honestly, Cath, and to be fair it was an easy thing for him to sort out. And I should be thanking *you*, for the wine, and the Christmas pudding.'

'Oh, nonsense, you're welcome. But listen, I was telling Sarah earlier about how Daniel helped us, and, well, I didn't realise he's actually looking for work in that field. He didn't mention that to Tony.'

'Oh!' Nicky gave a little laugh. 'No, that's not quite true, he isn't, not really. I don't know what Sarah said to you, but you see, he *wanted* to be a car mechanic – he's very good, his dad taught him – but, well, he has a full-time job in London now.'

'Oh.' Cath bit her lip. 'Oh dear, I hope haven't put my foot in it, then. I've sent Tony a message on my mobile, asking him to ring our son-in-law and tell him we know someone who might be able to help him. He's a farmer over the other side of Great Broomford, and he's looking for someone to sort out his old truck. I thought your Daniel might be able to help.'

'Well, he could probably have a look at it, at least,' Nicky said. 'But it's really just a hobby for him, you see. He might be able to give your son-in-law some advice, as a favour, though.'

'No, no – if he can *fix* it, my son-in-law will pay him properly. But of course, he's probably too busy, working all week.'

'Well, perhaps he might have time over the weekend,' Nicky said, looking a little brighter. 'I'll talk to him about it.'

'All right, dear. Let me know, will you?'

'Of course I will.' Nicky smiled, and I felt like smiling too. It sounded like good news. I hoped I was right for once.

*

I popped in next door to see them first thing in the morning, while they were getting ready for work.

'Well, are you up for it or not?' Nicky was saying as she ate a slice of toast, standing up, leaning against the kitchen worktop. 'We need to let Cath and Tony know.'

'I don't know, babe. It depends how much work it entails, doesn't it.'

I meowed with surprise. I was expecting Daniel to be really excited at the prospect of this working-on-a-truck thing. Especially being paid for it.

'For God's sake!' Nicky had obviously expected more excitement from him too. 'Just say you'll go and *look* at it and assess how much work it is – then you can decide whether you've got time or not. What's the matter? I thought you were really keen to get stuck into some motor work again?'

'I am!' He spread his hands, looking awkward. 'It's not about the time, Nick. If it's a lot of work, I could work all weekend, spread it over two weekends if necessary, or even take a couple of days' leave from the shop. I want to do it, and obviously I want the money . . .'

'So what's the problem?'

'I've hardly got any tools now. A lot of them were my dad's old stuff, but I'd got some things myself too. I left nearly all of them behind when I moved out. I couldn't exactly bring them all to your parents' place and expect them to store them somewhere. And of course, the next thing we heard was that Mum was selling up and moving to Spain with Whatsisname.'

'She surely didn't get rid of everything? Without even telling you? Oh, Dan! You never told me that,' Nicky said, looking appalled.

'By the time I'd phoned her and begged her to hang onto all the tools so that I could come and get what I wanted, it was too late. I was more upset because of them being Dad's, really. At that time I never thought I'd be working as a mechanic so I just had to put it behind me.'

'Oh.'

'Exactly: *Oh*. So is there really any point me even going all the way over there to look at the truck in the first place?'

'No. I suppose not.' She reached out and touched his hand. 'I'm so sorry, Dan.'

'Not your fault. I'll go and see them tonight and explain.'

'OK.'

They finished their cups of tea and slices of toast in silence and I left the house with them when they got into their little car to drive to the station at Great Broomford. Neither of them had spoken a word to me. I didn't blame them. I felt as disappointed as they were. Nothing seemed to be going the way I wanted, for some of my favourite humans. It didn't seem like I was going to be the Cat Who Saved Christmas for them at all.

CHAPTER
TWENTY ONE

I spent most of that day with Tabby again. He was feeling fed up because the pretty little Burmese he had his eye on wasn't interested in him.

'Why these pedigree females seem to think they're too good for the likes of us, I can never understand,' he complained. 'They should realise they'd have healthier kittens if they mated with good strong moggies like us, instead of going in for all that inbreeding.'

'I don't think you're going to be able to change the way of world just to suit your sex life, Tabs.'

'More's the pity. Anyway, how are things with you? Got over that business at the Big House now?'

'Yes. I'm just disappointed all our efforts didn't work.'

'All *your* efforts, you mean. I didn't even have a clue what you were up to, playing with bits of paper when we should have been legging it out of there.'

'It just seems such a shame. *She* likes him, and *he* seems to like her, too. Why can't they just get together and be happy?'

'Perhaps one of them is a pedigree and the other one isn't,' he said morosely. 'As you said, you can't change the world.'

No, I couldn't, and I was beginning to realise that.

We played together in Tabby's garden for a while, but we were both getting cold, and then suddenly it started to pour with that icy stuff they call sleet. It's the worst stuff of all, when it comes down hard, little Charlie. Drenches your fur and freezes it at the same time.

'Quick, into the garage,' he meowed at me. It was a lot closer than his cat flap. 'There's a gap under the door.'

I'd never been in there before. The gap where the door didn't close properly was only just big enough – I was surprised Tabby could squeeze through – but once inside, it was nice and dry, even if not very warm. We both sat and washed ourselves and rubbed our faces with our paws to get the icy drips off.

'Why have they got a garage,' I asked Tabby, looking around, 'if they haven't got a car?'

'They used to have one – a big old thing, it was. Very bad-tempered. It used to growl and cough a lot, and some-times it refused to move at all. They got rid of it in the end. Said they were getting too old to drive anyway, and now they just go on the bus or walk. My man, Eddie, used to look after it really well, too. See all those tools, in those boxes at the back there? He was forever opening the car's mouth and looking at its teeth or whatever was wrong with it. But he said he was getting too old to do that any more, too.'

'Oh.' A little idea was blooming in my head, as I'm sure you can guess. 'So why has your man still got all those tools?'

'Don't ask me. My woman said ages ago he should get rid of them, but you know what male humans are like, Ollie – never get around to anything. She did say the other day she was going to write an advert out to sell them, if he wouldn't do it.'

'And did she? Did she write the advert?'

'I don't know, Ollie. There's a bit of paper in the front window, but don't ask me what it is. I might be clever but I'm not Wonder-Cat, I can't read. Why are you so interested, anyway?'

'Oh, just being curious,' I said.

'Careful. You know what they say.'

'Yes, I do. And it hasn't killed me yet!'

I saw the piece of paper when we walked round the front of his house later. It was just ordinary white paper with big black letters on. For all I knew, it could be a page out of a newspaper. But was it worth a try? Or would I just be wasting my time – again?

After school that afternoon, Rose went to play with one of the children in her class. Grace went up to their bedroom, and when she came back down she was holding the pink purse, the one she'd tipped the money out of before.

'Mummy,' she said, 'can I ask you something? It's got to be a secret from Rose.'

I couldn't help letting out a little mew of anxiety. Was this it? Was this the point when they'd go and buy the new cat?

'What is it, love?' Sarah said, sounding amused. 'Have you decided what to get her for Christmas?'

'Well, yes, it could be her Christmas present. That would be good. But do you think I've got enough money yet?' She unzipped the purse and tipped out the coins and the note again. 'If Daddy gives me this week's pocket money tonight . . .'

'What is it you want to buy her? It doesn't have to be something expensive, Grace. It's the thought that counts.'

'A new cat. I want to buy her a new cat that she can call Sooty again.'

Sarah's eyes went wide with surprise. 'Oh, Grace, darling, that really isn't a good idea,' she said. 'I mean, it's sweet of you to think of it, but . . .'

'Why not?' Grace demanded crossly. 'I want to, Mum. I want to make up for being a horrible sister.'

Sarah put both paws round Grace and pulled her close. 'You're *not* a horrible sister, not at all. Why on earth would you think that?'

'I said that nasty thing to her, didn't I, that day when we got the Christmas tree? About her being stupid for running into the road to save Sooty. I don't know why I said it, Mummy. I was just feeling cross and impatient about decorating the tree.'

'Sweetheart, we all knew you didn't mean it. Even Rose knew you didn't. It's all forgotten now.'

'*I* haven't forgotten it,' Grace retorted. 'It still makes me feel horrible, knowing I said it.'

'Well, that just shows you're really a very nice sister, who wouldn't normally dream of hurting Rose's feelings. We all say nasty things sometimes, and feel sorry afterwards. But once you've *said* sorry, and been forgiven, Grace, you have to move on and forget about it.'

'OK.' Grace shrugged. 'But I still want to buy her a new cat.'

'We have Oliver now, don't we?'

Phew. I started to breathe again.

Grace frowned. 'But Oliver isn't really ours, not to keep, is he. I know Rose loves him – so do I – but when he gets taken back by his real owner, she's going to be even more upset.'

Sarah looked at her for a minute as if she was considering it.

'Well, you have got a point there . . .'

Oh no, I thought. *Here we go.*

'. . . and Daddy and I have already agreed we'll get another cat of our own after Oliver leaves. But perhaps you're right. Perhaps it should be before rather than after.'

She paused and glanced over at me, and I meowed loudly in distress.

'But I don't think it would be fair on Ollie,' she went on, 'to bring another cat into the house while he's staying with us.'

I wanted to rush over and jump on her lap and lick her to death, but I was almost too weak with relief to move.

'Oh, but *Mummy* . . .'

'We'll get a kitten instead.'

'Oh! A kitten! Oh, yes, that'd be even better.' Grace jumped up and punched the air as if she was one of those football people on the television. 'Have I got enough money for a *kitten*, then?' she added.

'Put your purse away, Grace,' Sarah said, laughing. 'Daddy and I will buy the kitten, but not until after Christmas. Christmas isn't the right time to bring a new pet into the house. No, don't argue, or I'll change my mind and we won't get one at all. There's too much excitement, and things going on. A kitten will need calm, and quiet, to settle down. After New Year, I promise you and Rose can *both* help to choose a kitten. So there's no need to keep it a secret from Rose. It'll be something for us all to look forward to. But why don't we go to the shop now, while Rose is out, and you can choose a book or a puzzle for her instead, that you can wrap up for her for Christmas?'

'OK. It *will* be exciting to have a new kitten to look forward to, won't it? Will Ollie mind that, though?'

'I don't think so. A kitten won't be a threat to him, like an adult cat might be, and it'll be more likely to accept that Oliver is Top Cat while he's here.'

They both looked at me. I was purring. A *kitten*! Oh, that would be nice. I could help to bring it up. It would be fun. And, most importantly, they obviously weren't planning to send me packing. I'd be Top Cat. I jumped out of my chair, stretched, and gave a big yawn of contentment, and Sarah and Grace both burst out laughing.

'It's almost like he's been listening,' Grace said, coming over to pick me up. 'Ah, Ollie, we still love you too, don't we, Mummy?'

'Of course we do,' Sarah agreed, giving me a stroke.

So I was one very happy, very lucky, cat, after all.

I'd have liked to stay with them that evening, cuddled up on the children's laps while they talked excitedly about our new kitten. But, of course, I had a plan involving Daniel next door, and now I was feeling more positive about life, I wanted to try it out, even though most of my plans seemed to be backfiring.

'Hello, Ollie!' Nicky said brightly when she opened the door to my usual chorus of meows. I'd tried to time it right so that they'd had their dinner but not settled down for the evening yet. 'Come in, out of the cold.'

'No!' I meowed. '*You* come out *here*.'

'Come on, boy,' she insisted. 'Quickly, we've got the fire lit and you're letting in the cold.'

I paraded up and down, my tail erect, looking back at her.

'What's going on?' Daniel called from inside the cottage.

'It's Ollie. He's behaving really strangely. He won't come in – he keeps pacing up and down outside.'

Daniel appeared behind her, watching me over her shoulder.

'He did that to me once before,' he said thoughtfully. 'Remember? That time I told you I had the distinct impression he wanted to lead me to the notice board.'

'Yeah, right!' She laughed. 'What are you, now? The cat whisperer?'

'Maybe.' He shrugged, but he was still watching me. I flicked my tail harder and walked a few paces towards the corner of the road. 'OK, I might be losing my marbles, but I'm going to follow him, Nick. I'll just get my coat.'

'If I didn't know you better, Dan, I'd say you were using Ollie as an excuse to pop off down the pub,' Nicky said, still laughing.

'If there was even a pub to pop down to.' He kissed her quickly on the cheek. 'Won't be long.'

Nicky shut the door behind us, shaking her head.

'Come on, then,' I told him, leading the way. Thank God he was getting better at understanding cat body-language.

We were soon at Tabby's house. Fortunately there was a lamppost right outside, and the white sheet of paper was still glaring from the window. I stopped outside the gate, turning round and round on the spot, meowing.

'What is it, Ollie?' Daniel said, staring around him. 'What's wrong?'

For mewing out loud, I thought. *I'm going to have to lead him by the nose!*

I hopped up onto the low front wall and over onto Tabby's front path, and up to the window. Did I really need to jump up onto the windowsill? No. When I turned back to Daniel, he was staring at the paper. Hooray! Now I just had to hope it wasn't just a *Happy Christmas* decoration or a sign I'd heard about, saying *No Cold Calling* – whatever that meant.

'Well, I'll be damned,' Daniel muttered to himself. 'That could be interesting.'

Could it? Well, I hoped so. He certainly seemed keen. He opened the gate and marched up the path, gave a firm rat-a-tat to the door knocker and waited, looking at me and shaking his head as if he couldn't quite work me out.

'Hello?' Eddie, Tabby's human, stood in the doorway, staring at him. 'Can I help you?'

'Hello. I've just seen the notice in your window,' Daniel said. 'Garage contents to be disposed of? Tools? Um, I just wondered what kind of tools you're selling.'

'Selling?' Eddie laughed. 'Just clearing them out, mate. Well, my wife is – it was her that put the notice up. She's sick of me hoarding stuff I don't need. Can't blame her really. We haven't even got a car now, so why would I want to hold onto all the gear I used to work on the old banger with?'

'Tools for *car* maintenance?' Daniel squawked. He glanced at me again, his mouth open. 'Sorry, it's just such a coincidence. I could really do with some. Can I have a look? And would you by any chance take a cheque?'

Eddie clapped a paw on his shoulder, laughing. 'I told you, lad, I don't want anything for them. Take the lot, if you like – you'll be doing me a favour. They're not new, mind. The wife was all for throwing them out. But if they'll do you a turn, so much the better. Come and have a look. Live in the village, do you? Haven't seen you around.'

And they disappeared round the side of the house to the garage, Daniel starting to tell Eddie where he lived, how recently he and Nicky had moved in, and how he'd got the offer of the work on the farmer's truck. By the time Daniel returned home, whistling, telling Nicky he needed to take the car round the corner because he'd got a box of heavy tools to bring back, I was on the chair next to Nicky, pretending to be asleep.

Mission accomplished. For once I'd been a success. What a good day. Suddenly I was feeling *much* better about myself.

CHAPTER
TWENTY TWO

When I went into Nicky and Daniel's house on my regular visit the next evening, I noticed that Daniel kept giving me funny looks.

'I really think there's something spooky about him,' he said to Nicky. 'He must have supernatural powers.'

She burst out laughing. It was nice to hear her sounding more cheerful.

'Oh, Dan, don't keep on about it! It was just a lucky coincidence. Save the fairy stories for after the baby's born.'

He cuddled her and I purred around their legs happily.

'You *are* looking forward to the baby, then?' he asked her softly.

'Of course I am, in one way. If only I wasn't so worried about the financial situation.'

'I know,' he said. 'Well, let's just hope that now I've accepted this bit of work with the farmer, it might be a turning point. Perhaps our luck's going to change. Now I've got the tools, I could even put a notice up on that board, offering to look at people's car problems, or do maintenance work.'

'That's a good idea. Just don't take on too much, though, Dan – you've only got weekends.'

Just at that moment, the doorbell rang, and Daniel went to answer it.

'It's someone for you,' he said to Nicky as he showed the visitor in.

It was Louise, one of the pram females. I meowed a hello to her and she smiled at me.

'Sorry to intrude,' she began, after Nicky had got up to greet her. 'And I hope you're not going to be offended . . .'

Nicky shook her head, looking puzzled.

'Sit down, please, Louise. Why would I be offended?'

'Well, Sarah had a little chat with me about you the other night. You probably heard I'm absolutely desperate for someone to look after my children.'

'Oh.' Nicky went bright red. 'I'm sorry. Sarah really shouldn't have said anything. I've already told her, I can't help you. It's not that I don't want to . . .'

'Don't be cross with Sarah. She was only trying to help – help both of us. She's obviously very fond of you, and she told me about your qualifications and your career so far, which I must say are really impressive.'

'Well, thank you, but you see, I already have a full-time position in London which, to be honest, pays good money and I need – Daniel and I need – that level of income.' She sounded really flustered and awkward. 'And I'm pregnant now,' she added. 'So I'm afraid it's out of the question.'

'Um, I know she probably shouldn't have,' Louise said, looking down at her paws, 'but Sarah did mention that to me, too. And it's all the more reason to work part-time, isn't it?' she added gently. 'Especially if it means there wouldn't be any commuting.'

'I know, but . . .'

'And especially if I offer to match what you're earning in London, minus your fares, so that overall you'll be no worse off.'

'What?' Nicky stared at her. 'I'm sorry, but I don't think you understand. I'm full-time at the nursery.'

'Yes, and I'm sure the money is excellent, for a nursery. But working as a private nanny, with your qualifications and background, you could almost demand your own salary. Dave and I earn good money too, Nicky, and good childcare is top of our priorities. I work twenty hours a week, but by the time I drive to work and back, I'll need you there for more like twenty-five. I might want the occasional couple of hours for an evening out, too,' she added, smiling. 'You realise you could make a little bit more around the village like that? Babysitting? I know of at least one other mum who's desperate for a good babysitter so that she and her husband can go out sometimes.'

'Oh.' Nicky glanced at Daniel, whose eyes were wide with surprise. 'Well, I don't know what to say. If it wasn't for the fact that I'll have my own baby . . .'

'That's exactly why you should go for it, Nick,' Daniel said. 'I've been really worried about the idea of you travelling up to London with the baby, working all day up there like that.'

'But how soon would you want me to start? I mean, the baby's due in May, and I'd have to have at least a couple of weeks off, I suppose.'

'I've thought about that. I've already spoken to my mum, and she'd be happy to cover while you take some maternity leave. Dave and I would take some holiday in the summer, too. I realise you'll want to talk this all over.' She hesitated. 'The thing is, I'd need someone to start as soon as possible after Kay retires at New Year. If you think there's even a chance you might be interested, please come and meet the children. Freya's quite a sensible little girl but she's not four till the middle of September, so she misses out on starting school this year – which means I'll need childcare for her for another whole year after that. And Henry, well, he doesn't seem to be turning out to be *too* demanding, as toddlers go.'

'I'm sure I've dealt with a lot worse at the nursery,' Nicky said, smiling. 'But you really wouldn't mind me having my own baby with me at the same time?'

'I think the kids would love it. And as long as you can cope, which I'm sure you'll be able to, by the sound of your current job, it'll be fine with me.' She sat back in her chair and took a deep breath. 'Will you at least consider it?'

'Well.' Nicky turned to Daniel, who was nodding enthusiastically. 'Yes, obviously it does sound interesting.'

'Then let's talk money,' Louise said, producing her phone from her bag and turning it into one of those adding-up things humans use instead of counting in their heads. 'And then I'll leave the two of you to talk it over.'

After she'd gone, there was a different atmosphere in the little cottage. Daniel and Nicky both seemed too stunned to talk, for a while.

'I said maybe our luck was changing,' Daniel said eventually.

'You think it could work? Honestly? It just seems too good to be true.'

'You haven't met her kids yet,' he teased her. 'They might be little demons.'

'I'm used to those,' she laughed. 'Oh, Dan, do you *really* think this might be a turning point?'

'I do, Nick. I think you should go for it. And an occasional bit of babysitting in someone's nice warm house for an evening – that wouldn't be so bad either, would it?'

'No, it wouldn't. I don't know why I didn't think of that myself. I could advertise that on the board, couldn't I?'

And they started hugging and kissing again. They didn't look like they wanted me to join in, so I jumped into the armchair nearest the fire and left them to it.

I was so cheered up by events in Nicky and Daniel's house, I made a rather rash decision. Despite everything, I was going back to the Big House. I wasn't going to tell Tabby this time – I knew he wouldn't come with me again anyway – but I couldn't get rid of this niggling feeling that I'd be letting Caroline down if I stayed away. From what I'd overheard, her father didn't let her have any friends in to play, and as well as being poorly and weak she must be so lonely, it made me mew with sadness just to think about her. At least I'd made her smile when I visited her. I told myself that, this time, I'd be far more careful. I already knew to avoid weekends, and now I'd avoid early mornings too in case the father was still there.

So the next day, I waited until Sarah stopped her work on the computer and started making herself a sandwich for lunch. I knew that meant it must be the middle of the day. I ran all the way up the hill to the Big House and up the driveway. The male called Harry was outside one of the sheds, sawing wood, but he had his back to me and I scampered straight across to the big windows, where I could see Caroline and Laura sitting in the room. I scratched at the glass with my paws and did some frantic meowing, and Caroline sat up, looking so excited to see me, I was already glad I'd come. Laura came over and opened the door.

'Oliver,' she said. 'You mustn't come here any more. You got us into a lot of trouble before.'

'But Daddy's not here now,' Caroline said, reaching out a paw towards me. '*Please* let Oliver come in again, Laura. He's never going to find out.'

'No, really, I don't think so.'

'Oh, *please*. It's so unfair. Daddy treats me like a prisoner. At least in hospital I could see the other children on the ward. Sometimes I wish I was still *in* hospital.'

'You don't mean that, Caroline,' Laura said, sounding upset.

'Don't I? I didn't like being so ill, but at least it wasn't *boring*.'

For a minute, Laura stood there in the doorway, blocking my entrance, looking down at me but blinking fast like she had dust in her eyes.

'OK, Oliver,' she muttered suddenly, standing back so that I could run inside. 'If he finds out, and starts on me again like last time, he can have my notice.'

I didn't know which notice she was talking about. One of the ones on the notice board, I supposed. I didn't care. I was just glad to be in the warm, cuddling up to Caroline again and seeing her smile.

So now I reasoned I was safe to go back to the Big House again, as long as I went in the middle of the day. And Caroline and I had such a lovely time in that nice warm room with the thick carpet and the comfy sofa. We played with a cotton reel, and a pencil tied to a length of string. Despite all the sophisticated cat toys your humans might buy you, Charlie, you can't beat a good old-fashioned bit of string for some jumping up with all four paws off the floor, or some rolling on your back with your paws in the air. You know the kind of thing. When Caroline got tired, we snuggled together on the sofa under the pink blanket and listened to Laura reading us a story. I was just happy to be allowed to cheer her up again.

That Saturday, I didn't see much of Daniel, because he'd gone off with his new box of tools in his car, to work on the farmer's truck. I spent a bit of time with Nicky to keep her company. She seemed happier. She told me she'd been round to Louise and Dave's house to meet their children, and that they seemed 'lovely'.

'We've decided I'm going to accept the job, Ollie,' she said, giving me a hug. 'Oh, I do hope we're doing the right thing. I've got to hand in my notice at the nursery. I feel a bit sick thinking about it, but Dan says it's going to be the best thing for me and the baby, and I'm sure he's right. It's just such a big change. I can still hardly believe I'm doing it. I wonder what my parents will say,' she added in a different tone of voice. 'They're bound to think I'm mad to give up such a good job.'

I was still at their house, asleep in the chair nearest the fire again, when Daniel finally arrived home just as it was getting dark.

'You must be worn out,' Nicky sympathised. 'Did you manage to finish the job?'

'Yep, all done, road tested and left in perfect running order,' he said happily, pulling off his boots. 'The guy was so pleased, he not only paid me, he's promised us a free turkey too.'

'A free *turkey*?' Nicky echoed.

'Yes, he's a poultry farmer. I've got to pick it up on Christmas Eve. It'll be plucked and oven ready for us.'

'Oh, Dan, that's wonderful. I'd been doing a reckon-up of our bills and trying to work out whether we could afford to get a cheap one from the supermarket.'

'This'll be much nicer, Nick, and bigger. It'll last us all week. Now we've got the turkey, the pudding and the wine,' he said, giving her a hug. 'I wonder what I can get from my next client.'

She laughed. 'Well, don't count your chickens – or should I say your turkeys. You haven't got another client *yet*. Although, if you put that advert up . . .'

'Actually,' he said, a note of pride in his voice, 'I've got another job lined up already. Rob, the farmer, has recommended me to a friend of his. He's a gardener and

258

handyman whose van needs a bit of attention. Should be a quick, easy job. I've got a day's leave to take before Christmas so I'll book him in in a couple of days' time.'

'Oh, Dan, that's amazing. Each job has led to another one. You must be doing something right.'

'Well, it's made me realise how nice people are, around here. They're all saying they like to give work to local people and help each other. I'm just really grateful for the chance to do a bit of my *tinkering* again.'

'*And* get paid for it. Anyway, go and have a hot bath, and put those greasy clothes in the washing machine. I've got a shepherd's pie ready to go in the oven.'

'Lovely. I'm starving.' He kissed her. 'You're an angel.'

She giggled. 'And *you*'re freezing cold, and filthy dirty. Go on, clean up.'

He was whistling as he went upstairs. I was actually really pleased to hear it.

So a couple of days later, when I was making my way up the drive of the Big House to play with Caroline, I noticed a car parked by the garage that looked exactly like Daniel's. When I got a bit closer, I nearly jumped in the air with surprise. It *was* Daniel's! And there he was, standing just inside the garage doors, talking to the man called Harry. I hid under a shrub and wriggled closer so that I could hear what they were saying.

'Really pleased you could fit me in so quickly, mate,' Harry said. 'Rob told me you did a fantastic job on his truck. Good to know there's someone in the village now that we can call on. Been in the business long, have you?'

'Well, to be honest,' Daniel said, 'it's not my full time job. Kind of a sideline, really.'

'Pity. I bet you'd get a lot of work around here if you set yourself up in business. There's no one else local, and who wants to take their car to those rip-off big companies in town? Anyway, look, the van just needs a tune-up for now, but there's a bit of bodywork damage here that I wouldn't mind getting sorted out at some point. Do you get involved with that? Panel beating and respraying?'

'Absolutely,' Daniel said, sounding so excited, anyone would think he'd been offered a bowl of meaty-chunks. 'Would you like me to quote you for doing that, while I'm here?'

'Yeah, would you do that, please, mate? I'd be glad to get it done. Right, I'll leave you to it, then – I've got to get on. His Lordship wants some holly and ivy cut today to decorate the place for Christmas. And there's a Christmas tree to carry indoors. Bloody Jack-of-all-trades here, I am. Still, he's generous with the pay, so I've got no complaints.'

He turned in my direction to head towards the wooded area of the grounds, just as I'd sneaked out from under my shrub to run across the lawn to the house.

'Morning, Oliver,' he called out cheerfully.

Laura had obviously let him in on the secret that I was visiting again. The angry father wouldn't be there today, I was sure of it, but for a minute I froze, looking from him to Daniel and back again, swishing my tail anxiously.

'Ollie!' Daniel said in surprise. 'What are *you* doing here?'

'Is he your cat?' Harry asked.

'No, he belongs to the pub, but my neighbour and I are looking after him, between us, until it's rebuilt. I didn't realise he wandered this far.'

'Oh yes. We keep it quiet, mind.' Harry laughed. 'He comes to visit Caroline.'

'Who?'

'The daughter. She's been ill, in hospital for ages – leukemia, poor kid. On the mend now, but her father's kind of over-protective. He went potty when he found out Laura – that's the nurse he's hired for Caroline – had been letting the cat in. Thinks they carry germs, or something. But Oliver cheers the kid up so much, Laura gave in and let him in again. Caroline's lonely, you see. She doesn't see a soul, stuck in this house all day every day. For God's sake keep this to yourself, or Laura will probably lose her job.'

'Right.' Daniel was staring at me. 'Somehow, that's just typical of Ollie, wanting to cheer up a lonely child. He's quite a special kind of cat.'

'Thanks! Nice to be appreciated,' I meowed at him. And then I ran off quickly to the house, to be let in out of the cold. Special cat or not, I needed my home comforts.

CHAPTER
TWENTY THREE

That evening, Sarah and Martin cleared up the dinner things early and got the children to bed. Nicky and Daniel were coming in for drinks again, and there was a kind of excitement in the air.

'Nicky said they've got some good news,' Sarah said. 'Oh, I do hope things are improving for them, Mart.'

So a bit later I sat in my hammock on the radiator, happily washing myself, as Nicky explained how she'd now accepted Louise's offer and was leaving the nursery after Christmas to start as nanny to Freya and Henry.

'I have to thank you, Sarah,' she said, looking slightly embarrassed for a moment. 'I understand you put in a good word for me. I'm sorry I was snappy with you when you tried to encourage me to talk to her. I really didn't expect her to offer me such a good deal.'

'I'm just pleased it's working out for you,' Sarah said. 'Congratulations. They're nice children, too. I'm sure you've made the right decision.'

'And it helps that I've been earning a bit extra,' Daniel said. 'Doing a little bit of work on some motors. Actually, I have Ollie to thank for that.'

'Dan believes Ollie's got magic powers,' Nicky giggled. 'He thinks he somehow knew this guy called Eddie had some tools to get rid of, and led him to his house.'

They all turned to look at me. I lifted my head and meowed, and they all burst out laughing.

'Magic powers, indeed,' scoffed Martin. 'Look at him. He's just a shy little pussy cat.'

'Well, I don't know about that,' Daniel said. 'Guess where I saw him today?'

I froze, mid-wash. Daniel had been warned about keeping my visits secret. I didn't want to get into trouble with the angry father, or get Laura into trouble with him, either. But he was tapping the side of his nose with a finger as he went on:

'This is strictly between us, mind. I've taken a vow of silence about it.'

And he explained about his job at the Big House, and what Harry had told him, about Caroline, and Laura, and the father's dislike of cats.

'I didn't even know he had a daughter,' Sarah exclaimed. 'Not that we really know him. All I know is he's called Julian Smythe, and he hardly ever comes into the village, but on the few occasions he's been to the shop he's apparently been so grumpy and miserable, he's made himself unpopular.'

'Well, Harry said Caroline was in hospital for a long while after they moved here, and now the poor kid is holed up there all day every day, just her and the nurse. So she hasn't even been to school since they moved from London, and hasn't got any friends here.'

'Poor girl.' Sarah sighed. 'I don't suppose anyone else in the village knows about her either, then. How old did you say she is?'

'Ten, apparently.'

'Similar age to Grace. What a shame that she hasn't even got any friends to play with.'

'That seems to be why Ollie's been going up there. I'm telling you, there's something a bit *different* about that cat. He almost seems to understand humans.'

The others all laughed again, and I went back to washing myself, pretending not to take any notice. If only they knew, eh, Charlie? Nothing unusual in us cats understanding humans. It's them who can't understand us, more's the pity.

'There's another bit of news in the village, as it happens,' Sarah said a little later. She picked up her wine glass. 'Top up the drinks, can you, Mart? Remember Nicky's only on orange juice.'

'So what's the news?' he asked as he poured the wine.

'You know old Barbara Griggs down Back Lane? And I told you she and Stan Middleton have been spending time and laughing together?'

'Yes. Bloody amazing. I thought they were both cantankerous old devils. Maybe they're well suited.'

'It appears so.' Sarah paused for effect. 'Let's hope so, anyway. They're getting married!'

'What?' Martin nearly dropped the wine bottle. 'You're joking! They must both be getting on for ninety.'

'I know, but apparently they've become soul mates. One of the older ladies from the WI who goes to the pensioners' get-togethers told me Barbara is announcing it to the whole world.'

'Ah. I think that's rather sweet,' Nicky said. 'Bless them!'

'Bless them?' Martin retorted, laughing. 'Well, I suppose we should all be pleased they're getting along together and keeping each other quiet. That woman used to frighten the life out of us all, even when I was a kid. She used to shout at us if we rode our bikes past her house or made too much noise playing outside. We thought she was a witch.'

'Love must have had a calming effect on her,' Sarah giggled. 'Apparently she's being as nice as pie to everyone now. She's had her hair coloured, her nails painted and has started wearing lipstick.'

'Good for her,' Nicky said. 'When are they getting married?'

'Soon after New Year, apparently, at the church in Great Broomford. They seem to be in quite a hurry. Barbara told the other ladies on the quiet that Stan wanted them to move in together, to save on heating and council tax and so on. And she wouldn't hear of it unless he married her first.'

'Fair enough,' Daniel said. 'And anyway, it's not a bad idea, is it. They say two can live as cheaply as one.'

'If only that were true,' Nicky said, sighing. 'How about three living as cheaply as one?' she added, patting her tummy.

'You'll be fine,' Sarah comforted her. 'Things are looking up for you both. You'll see, it'll all come good, Nicky. I'm sure of it.'

*

Hearing them talking about Nicky and Daniel's baby, reminded me that I hadn't seen Tabby or Suki for a few days, so the next morning before going on my visit to the Big House, I trotted round to Tabby's place and meowed loudly at his cat flap until he finally put his head through, looking like he'd just woken up.

'All right, keep your fur on,' he said crossly. 'What's up?'

'Nothing! I was just wondering how you were, but if you're in a bad mood I'll go away again.'

'Sorry.' He jumped through the flap to join me. 'Suki turned up last night and gave me a right earful. I've been sleeping off my headache ever since.'

'I thought you said she'd calmed down a bit since we had that chat with her?'

'She had. But it seems her humans have realised she's pregnant now.'

'Oh dear. Were they upset with her?'

'Not really. Suki said they blamed themselves for letting her out at night without getting her spayed.'

'I see.'

'So they're saying that as soon as she's recovered from having the kittens, and she's weaned them, they're going to take her to the vet's. She's heard from one of her friends that it's a really big operation for females. So now she's blaming me for that too. She says *I* should have been done. *It's just a little snip for a male,* she said. Like it's *my* fault my humans didn't take me to the vet like yours did.'

'If they had, you wouldn't have wanted to mate with her in the first place,' I reminded him.

'Hmm. Well, maybe that wouldn't have been such a bad thing,' he muttered. 'It just leads to trouble, if you want my opinion.'

I couldn't help laughing. Maybe now he wouldn't be in such a hurry to mate with every available female he met.

'What about the kittens, then?' I asked. 'Are Suki's humans going to look after them?'

'Well, they said they'll keep one – which will be nice for Suki. It'll keep her busy and maybe she'll leave me alone. And they'll let the others go to new homes. I think they'll probably advertise them for sale after they're weaned.'

'Perhaps your Eddie will buy one to keep *you* busy?' I teased him.

'Huh!' He turned his back on me, twitching his tail. 'What would I do with a kitten? If *you* want one, get your own humans to buy one.'

'As it happens, they're already talking about getting one,' I said. 'And, do you know what? You've just given me an idea.'

I had to be careful how I did it. From what Tabby had said about Suki's angry mood, I didn't want to do anything to upset her. I called on her straight after saying goodbye to him.

'Oh, hello, Ollie,' she said, looking up from washing her tummy. It wasn't surprising that her humans had noticed her pregnancy. She was looking bigger every time I saw her. 'Nice to see you.'

'Is it?' I squeaked in surprise. 'I mean, sorry, nice to see you, too. How are you keeping?'

'Not bad. I suppose Tabby sent you round? I was a bit hard on him last night. I suppose I'm taking it out on him, but can you blame me?'

'No, I can't blame you, Suki. But he didn't send me round. He doesn't know I've come. Look, I hear your humans are only going to let you keep one of your kittens?'

'Yes.' She sighed. 'Don't get me wrong – one will be more than enough, really. It'll be hard work feeding them all until they're weaned, never mind keeping an eye on them once they start running around. But, you know, they *will* be my own flesh and blood. Well, mine and Tabby's, more's the pity.'

'I expect you'd like them to go to nice human families, wouldn't you?'

'Yes. Of course – I wouldn't want them to go to humans who don't look after them properly, obviously.'

'Well, look, I've got a suggestion. Obviously you don't know how many kittens you're going to have, but I can at least try to get one of them into a lovely family.'

'How come?'

'It's my foster family. They're getting a kitten some time after Christmas. So . . . how can I put this nicely, Suki? Why don't you come home with me this evening and show them your tummy?'

It took a while for Sarah and Martin to catch on. Sarah was surprised, of course, to see me on the doorstep with Suki.

'Oh! Who's this?' she said. 'Martin! I think Ollie's brought a friend home.'

'Really? Well, they can play outside, then. I don't mind, but if we start letting all the neighbourhood cats in, there's no knowing where it'll end – especially if they all want to bring dead pigeons home with them.'

He followed Sarah to the front door and looked down at us.

'Roll on your back,' I hissed at Suki. 'Go on!'

She gave me a bit of a look, but did it anyway. I saw Martin's face change.

'That's not just a friend,' he said quietly. 'If I'm not much mistaken, it's a girlfriend.'

'She looks like she's pregnant,' Sarah agreed.

'But I thought . . . I'm sure George said Ollie had been neutered.'

What? 'It's nothing to do with *me*!' I meowed at them indignantly. Perhaps I should have marched Tabby round there too.

'You're right, he's neutered,' Sarah said. 'That's why he's so sweet.'

Now it was Martin's turn to look indignant! I wasn't sure I liked being called *sweet*, but I was too relieved that they realised I wasn't responsible for Suki's condition to make a big meow about it.

'So your friend's got herself in a bit of a fix, has she, Ollie?' Martin said, grinning. 'Oh well. She's obviously from a good home. She's beautiful, isn't she?'

'So Tabby seems to think,' I said.

'Have a look at her collar, Mart,' Sarah suggested. 'Let's just make sure she's not lost, or anything.'

Suki stood up and allowed Martin to look at her identity disc.

'Oh, she lives at The Willows, down Ponds Farm Road. Her name's Suki. Hello, Suki. You're a lovely girl, aren't you?'

'That's Arthur and Joan Furlong's place, isn't it?' Sarah said. 'You know them, they used to run the café in Great Broomford before they retired. The Singing Kettle, next to the church. Nice couple – I think he's got quite bad arthritis now so they don't get out much. Never knew they had a cat. Wonder what they're going to do with the kittens.'

I looked at Suki, she looked at me, and we both meowed. Sarah laughed.

'I have an idea,' she said. 'Shall we ask them if they're planning to sell them? You know I promised Grace we could get a new kitten after Christmas.'

'Yes.' Martin nodded thoughtfully. 'It would save us going to the Cats' Protection League, wouldn't it?'

'And if her kittens take after Suki, they're going to be gorgeous.'

Suki stretched her neck and purred, making Sarah laugh again.

'Yes, you know you're beautiful, don't you,' she said, bending down to stroke her. I almost felt jealous, but only for a minute, because then she added: 'You're a clever boy,

Ollie, bringing Suki home with you. Anyone would think you knew we'd be interested in her kittens.'

'Perhaps Daniel's right, after all,' Martin chuckled. 'Perhaps Ollie really does have magical powers.'

Perhaps I did. You know what, Charlie? I was almost beginning to think so myself.

CHAPTER
TWENTY FOUR

CHAPTER
TWENTY FOUR

Hello again, Charlie. You know, I'm surprised you keep asking to hear more of my story. I'd have thought a little kitten like you would have been bored with it by now. You say you think it's exciting? Well, thank you, I suppose it must be the way I'm telling it. Anyway, if you want to hear the rest – yes, we're coming to the end soon! – you'd better settle down and leave your tail alone. It's not going anywhere, it'll still be there to chase when I've finished.

Now, at this point in my story we were getting really close to Christmas. I could tell by the ever-increasing levels of excitement in Sarah and Martin's house. Apparently there were only a couple of days left at school, because Grace came running downstairs the next morning, singing at the top of her voice:

'Hooray, hooray, hooray, it's nearly the holiday!'

But instead of feeling excited, I felt sad. George had said he'd be back again to see us before Christmas, hadn't he, and now I was wondering whether he wasn't coming after all. Had he forgotten all about me? Decided he'd got used to not having a cat and wouldn't bother to have me back when the pub was mended? I mewed to myself miserably at the thought of it.

'What's wrong, Ollie?' Sarah asked. 'Cheer up, it's nearly Christmas!'

I didn't feel like cheering up. But I supposed I should go and see Caroline as usual and cheer *her* up, at least. I waited until Sarah was having her lunch, and then meowed a goodbye as I popped out of the cat flap and set off for the Big House.

Caroline didn't look particularly cheerful either, although Laura was doing her best to sound bright and chirpy. The room looked lovely, with a really big Christmas tree like we used to have in the pub, and lots of pretty decorations, but Caroline had a long face like a cat with a toothache.

'I'm so *bored*,' she moaned.

'But Oliver's come to play with you,' Laura said.

'I know. But I want *friends* to play with. It's not fair. I never get to see *anyone*. When can I start the new school? I won't have any friends there – nobody will know me.'

'You'll soon make friends when you're well enough to go. Hopefully before too long.'

We played together as usual, although Caroline didn't quite seem to have her heart in it and I found it difficult to keep myself from jumping up and having a play with the baubles on the lower branches of the Christmas tree. I did manage one quick swipe while Laura wasn't looking, but Caroline whispered *No, Oliver, you mustn't!* so I reluctantly left it alone. Then, just as we'd both snuggled down for our rest, there was a sudden loud banging noise that made me jump up out of Caroline's blanket in fright. At least it made her giggle.

'It's only the door knocker, Oliver!' she said. 'Who's that, Laura?'

'I've no idea.'

Laura left the room, and I hid back under the blanket. I was still supposed to be a secret, remember, and we'd never had other visitors before when I was there. We both lay quietly, listening to Laura talking to someone at the front door.

'Oh!' she was saying. 'Well, that's very kind of you. Um . . . did Mr Smythe tell you about her illness? Only, I know he doesn't talk to many people about it.'

'No,' said the other voice – and I popped my head out of the blanket in surprise. It was Sarah! 'To be honest, we heard . . . from another source. I don't want to get anyone into trouble for gossiping or anything, if it's supposed to be kept quiet, but, well, we felt so sorry for the little girl – being ill, and new to the area, not having any friends. Especially at this time of the year.'

'You're very kind,' Laura said again. 'Would you like to come in and meet Caroline?'

'Are you sure that'd be all right?'

'Well, *I* think it'd be nice for her. She'd love to have some visitors.'

Caroline and I were blinking at each other in surprise. And the next thing we knew, there they were, in the room with us – not just Sarah but also Grace, and little Rose, still in their school uniforms, and clutching some wrapped-up parcels!

'It's Ollie!' Grace said, staring at me.

'Yes.' Sarah smiled. 'We heard he'd been visiting.'

'Oh, so *you're* the family he's staying with! Harry – our handyman – said he'd found out Oliver was the pub cat

279

and was being looked after for the landlord since the fire.'
Laura reached out and stroked my head. 'Caroline loves
seeing him. But I'm afraid I'd get into trouble with her
father if he found him here again.'

'We won't tell anyone, will we, children,' Sarah said very
seriously, and they both shook their heads. They were
staring at Caroline. I suppose they were surprised by the
lack of fur on her head.

'It's all right,' she said, sitting up on the sofa. 'My hair
fell out because of the medicine they gave me to make me
better, but it's starting to come back now.'

'So *are* you better now?' Rose asked shyly.

'Getting better,' Caroline said. 'I'm just bored now.'

'These are for you.' Grace held out one of the wrapped-
up boxes. 'They're for Christmas, from us.'

'Oh!' Caroline went all pink. 'Thank you! Should we
put them under the Christmas tree, Laura?'

'You can open them now if you'd like to,' Sarah said.
'If Laura says that's all right.'

Grace and Rose crowded round and the three girls
laughed together as the paper was ripped off the boxes. Me,
I had a great time rolling on the floor with the ribbon they'd
been tied up with, and jumping after the screwed-up wrapping paper, which made them all laugh even more. I think
we were all feeling more cheered up, then. Sarah and Laura
sat on the other sofa together drinking coffee and chatting,
and the girls played with the new toys and talked about
school and hospital and Christmas and Brownies – and
eventually I fell asleep in front of the fire. It was lovely. I

must have got there later than usual, and it was now at least halfway through the afternoon because the girls had finished school. But I didn't realise quite *how* late it was, until I woke up with a start to hear the front door opening.

'Oh my God!' Laura gasped, jumping to her feet. 'He's home early.'

'Shall we go?' Sarah asked – but there was no time for anyone, even me, to go anywhere. Caroline's angry father was already there, in the doorway, looking around at us all, going redder in the face every minute.

'What the hell . . .?' he began, but Laura went to stand in front of him, her paws on her hips.

'Don't start, Julian!' she said, in a very cross voice. 'Don't you *dare* start, in front of these kind people who've come, out of the goodness of their hearts, to visit your *bored*, *lonely* daughter and bring her these presents because they *understood* – yes, they understood better than you do – how she must be feeling.'

'What?' he stuttered.

'Yes! Look at her. *Look* at how happy she is, how much healthier she looks, just from having some company, some children to play with for a couple of hours. It's what she needs now, Julian, and I'm *not* going to apologise for allowing it, nor for allowing the cat to come back, either. He's living with this lovely family, and he's not dirty, or carrying germs, he's a nice little cat and he does Caroline good. If you don't like it, you'd better sack me right now, because I refuse to carry on keeping your daughter languishing here on her own for *one single day longer*.'

As she finished, she suddenly clasped her paw to her mouth and took a step backwards, like she'd only just realised who she was talking to. We all stood still, frozen like statues, staring at the Julian man.

'We'd better go,' Sarah said again. 'Come on, children.'

'No,' he said, putting out a paw to stop her. 'Don't.' His voice sounded like a cat being strangled. 'Please, don't rush off. It *was* kind of you to call on Caroline, and . . . thank you for the presents. Please don't think me horribly rude. I'm just . . .'

'He's just been worried about Caroline,' Laura said, in a shaky voice now, staring at him. 'That's all.'

'Yes. I have. Worried sick. But Laura's right. I'm sorry. I should have let Caroline have some company. I can see how much happier she looks today. I'm sorry, darling,' he added with a funny choking noise like he was going to cry – and he ran to take hold of Caroline and hug her really hard. 'I'll try to be different.'

'It's OK, Daddy,' she said. 'I know you were just trying to look after me. But I'm getting better now.'

'I know you are. Thank God.' He made the choking noise again. 'Her mother . . .' he added, looking up at Sarah. 'You see, I lost her mother, and then, when Caroline got sick too . . .'

'I'm so sorry to hear that,' Sarah said, putting a paw on his arm. 'It must have been an awful time for you. I'm so glad to hear Caroline's getting better, but if you'd prefer us not to come again . . .'

'No. Please – if I haven't frightened you off,' he said, with a little sad smile, 'please do bring the children again. Caroline *does* need to make friends, and Laura's right, it was kind of you to visit. Thank you.'

I followed Laura as she showed Sarah and the girls to the front door, apologising quietly for the *scene*, as she called it.

'Please don't worry,' Sarah said. 'I do understand.'

I took the opportunity to scoot out of the front door myself. But as they walked off down the drive, I slunk round to the big windows where I normally went in and out. I wanted to make sure Julian wasn't going to tell Laura off after everyone had gone.

But, to my surprise, there was a totally different kind of *scene* going on in the room. While Caroline was engrossed with her new Christmas toys, Julian put both front paws round Laura and pulled her very close to him. I couldn't hear what he was saying – he was talking right into her ear. But she was quite pink in the face and smiley. And his mouth was moving slowly down from her ear to her lips . . .

At least he didn't seem to be angry anymore. I went home feeling *much* happier!

It didn't take long for word to get around. Sarah got on the phone to Anne, the one they called Brown Owl, and next thing I knew, she turned up with a couple of the other Foxes and their mums, and everyone started chatting about how they could take the children to visit Caroline.

'I'm going to draw a picture for Caroline,' Rose said, getting out her crayons.

'I'm going to make her a Christmas card,' Grace said.

'Me too,' said one of the other Foxes, and the children all clustered around the table, sharing out paper and crayons and pens.

'We should stagger our visits,' Anne said. 'We don't want to overwhelm the poor child by all turning up together.'

'That's a good idea,' Sarah agreed. 'Let's get our diaries out and get ourselves organised.'

'It will be lovely for Caroline to make some friends before she starts school,' Anne said. 'And perhaps she'll be well enough to join Guides by the time Grace moves up. They can start together. Thank goodness her father's seen sense. She must have felt so isolated, poor thing.'

'I can understand it, though,' Sarah said. 'He was beside himself with worry about her. I don't think he's really a miserable person at all. He's just had a lot of unhappiness.' She grinned suddenly. 'But do you know what? I think that nurse, Laura, has a soft spot for him. And he might not show it, but I suspect he feels the same way.'

I lay back in my hammock, purring to myself with a secret happiness. I didn't know where Laura's *soft spot* might be, but I knew for sure that it was true they liked each other. I was the only one who'd seen the evidence with my own eyes.

CHAPTER
TWENTY FIVE

Later that evening, after dinner, I was paying my usual visit to Nicky and Daniel's house, when Sarah turned up to share the news with them about what had happened at the Big House.

'Poor little girl,' Nicky sympathised. 'But how lovely that you're taking all the children round there to play with her now.'

'Yes. I actually feel sorry for her dad, too, now.'

'I'll be meeting him myself soon,' Daniel said. 'I haven't had a chance to tell you this yet, Nick, but the handyman, Harry, apparently recommended me to him after I did the work on his van. Mr Smythe wants me to service his car. Well, he's actually got two cars – a Mercedes, and a smaller one he uses to commute to the station. Harry called me today to say he wants me to go over there after Christmas to talk to him about it.'

'Oh, well done, Dan, that's great.' Nicky gave him a kiss. 'Maybe he'll want them both serviced regularly – and you've got the bodywork on Harry's van to do, too.'

'I'm really pleased for you.' Sarah smiled. 'It all helps, doesn't it. And you enjoy doing it, anyway. Perhaps you'll have a look at our car when you get the chance. Martin keeps complaining that it turns over too slowly, or something.'

'Of course I will.' Daniel looked like the cat that got the cream. I knew exactly how that felt.

*

The next day was the children's last day at school, and Sarah brought them along to the Big House again after they'd finished. I was already there, of course, cuddled up with Caroline, and at first I was horrified to hear the Julian man coming home early again. But Laura and Caroline just smiled at each other and told Sarah that it was absolutely fine now, and he was home early because he' was doing something called *winding down for Christmas.*

Sure enough, he was like a completely different human. He came into the room full of smiles, giving Caroline a big hug and kiss, and touching Laura on her paw in a way that made me think he wanted to stroke her.

'Good to see you again,' he said to Sarah and the children. '*And* our little furry friend there.'

I nearly fell off the sofa in surprise. Was this really the same male who'd half-strangled me and called me a dirty, flea-ridden animal? I thought he hated cats?

'I actually quite like cats, you know,' he went on as if I'd spoken out loud in Human. 'At least, I used to, before I became so . . . well, overly obsessed with hygiene, I suppose, because of Caroline's illness.'

'Oh, Daddy, can we have one?' Caroline said. 'I love Oliver so much, and it's so lovely that he comes to see me, but he's not mine, and I'd *love* a little cat of my own.'

'Well, I don't know about that.' He frowned. 'I'll have to think about it. Maybe after Christmas.' He turned to Sarah, obviously keen to change the subject. 'Apparently some of the other little girls are coming to visit Caroline tomorrow. Children from the Brownie pack.'

288

'Yes. They're in the same Six as Grace and Rose.'

'Caroline's been so excited about it,' he said. 'She used to love Brownies, didn't you, darling?'

'Yes, Daddy. And I want to join *this* Brownie pack, now I've met Grace and Rose and heard all about it. Can I? Please?'

'We . . . e . . . ll . . .'

'She *is* getting stronger,' Laura said. 'Perhaps, after Christmas, I could take her along to a meeting, at least, and stay with her? She could just watch – she wouldn't have to run around or anything.'

'That would be lovely,' Sarah said, 'but the Brownies aren't having proper pack meetings now. We're just having meetings for each Six, separately, in each other's houses, because . . .'

'Oh, yes – because of the fire. Grace told me,' Caroline said. 'There's no village hall for them to meet in, Daddy.'

'Oh, of course, the pub fire. I'd forgotten the hall was damaged too.' He looked down at his paws. 'I'm afraid I don't often go into the village. I've found it difficult to meet people, to be honest. I didn't know how I'd handle it if they started asking questions, so I kept out of their way. I realise now how stupid that was. Everyone must have thought I was being stand-offish.'

'Oh, well, I wouldn't say that . . .' Sarah began, but her mouth was twitching at the corners.

He smiled and shrugged. He looked so much nicer when he smiled.

'I can't blame them. But now you and the children, and the other families, are being so good to us, I've realised, well . . .' He hesitated, then admitted, 'I guess it wasn't just Caroline who was desperately in need of some good neighbours. You must let me know if I can do anything in return.'

'There's no need, honestly. We're happy to help.'

'Thank you, again.' He turned to go. Halfway out of the door, he swung round and looked back at Sarah.

'So there's *nowhere* for all the Brownies to meet together? Nowhere else in the village?'

'No. Not just the Brownies. None of the groups and clubs have anywhere to meet. But it's funny how we've all somehow managed to get around it. People in the village have become so good at improvising and co-operating with each other – we've actually all benefited from the situation, in a way. Small groups have been getting together in each other's homes, drawing up rotas, even making new friends.'

'But we can't have a Christmas party this year,' Grace said sadly.

'No.' Sarah shook her head. '*All* the Christmas parties and meals have had to be cancelled. The pensioners, the WI, the playgroup, mums-and-babies group – obviously nobody has room to cater for the numbers that would be involved.'

'I see.' Julian paused, looking around him. 'But we do.'

'Pardon?'

'I said, *we* do.' His eyes went suddenly brighter, like he'd just seen a nice juicy mouse running past. 'We've got empty rooms in this house, rooms that I haven't even got around to furnishing. We've got an enormous great *ballroom*, for God's sake! *All* the clubs could have their parties in there, and it still probably wouldn't be crowded. In fact,' he went on, sounding so excited now, Caroline had sat upright in surprise, and Laura and Sarah both had their mouths hanging open, staring at him, 'in fact, why don't we just have the whole village here together? Make it a huge village family party? Let's do it! I've got a colleague who used to moonlight as a DJ – he's still got all his equipment. I know he'll do me a favour if I ask him. Let's start at teatime, so all the children can come. How about Christmas Eve? A lot of people will have finished work early.'

'Oh, Daddy!' Caroline was squealing. 'Can I come? Please, please, can I come? I won't even have to leave the house. And Laura will be here to look after me. And I can see Grace and Rose and the other Brownies.'

'Yes, of course you can. But you'll have to remember you still get very tired. You won't be able to run around like the other children.'

Caroline bounced up and down on the sofa, her cheeks all pink with excitement.

'But . . .' Sarah had gone a bit pink too. 'Mr Smythe, honestly, you can't . . .'

'*Julian*, for goodness' sake, and yes I can. I *want* to. It's the least I can do, to make up for being so unsociable and rude.'

'But what about food, Julian?' Laura asked, looking worried. 'It's such short notice. I mean, I'll help, but there's not much time for shopping or cooking.'

'Hmm, that's a point. Might be too late to organise caterers,' he said, frowning.

'Perhaps we should leave it until after Christmas,' Laura suggested.

'But I'd like to make it a Christmas party,' Julian insisted. 'Where's your sense of fun, Laura?' He laughed. 'It'll be great – spontaneous! I'll just have to drive into town and load up with lots of party food.'

'No!' Sarah stood up now, shaking her head. 'Absolutely not. If you really want to do this – and honestly, I agree it's a bit rushed! – we certainly can't let you go to the trouble and expense of providing food. There are too many of us. We'll sort it out together, like we've been doing, with notices on the notice board, and with phone calls, emails, and notes through people's doors, and we'll all bring something along. Plates of sausage rolls, sandwiches, cakes – everyone who comes will rustle up or buy something quickly.'

He started to protest, but Laura stopped him.

'It's actually a good idea, Julian,' she said. 'People won't feel so embarrassed about coming, if they contribute.'

'Oh, I suppose that's a point. All right, then, but please tell them the contributions are voluntary. And I'll provide drinks. Soft drinks for kids, wine and beer for the adults who want it. I insist! It's the first thing I've contributed to village life, and not before time.' He grinned at Laura. 'I'm looking forward to this. It's . . .' He coughed, and took a deep breath. 'It's the first thing I've looked forward to for a long while.'

'Perhaps the first of many,' Laura said quietly, and they gave each other that long look again.

'Oh, for goodness' sake, Daddy, why don't you just kiss her?' Caroline said. 'It's been obvious for ages that you want to.'

And everyone burst out laughing.

When Sarah was ready to leave, I decided to go with them. Grace and Rose lingered over their goodbyes to Caroline, while I followed Julian and Sarah out into the hall.

'Just a thought,' Sarah said very quietly to Julian. 'If you *do* decide to get Caroline a cat after Christmas, we happen to know someone whose cat's having kittens soon. We're actually getting one ourselves. We went to see the couple last night, and they'll be wanting to re-home all but one of the kittens. If you're sure about this party, and they come, I'll introduce you.'

'Thank you. Yes,' he said, 'I think, now I've got over the shock of seeing Oliver with her, it would be very good for Caroline. And I like the idea of having a kitten from someone in the village.'

'I'm glad. You know, a lot of what's happened here seems to have come about because of Oliver. Since he's been with us, things seem to have . . . fallen into place, somehow.' She laughed. 'My neighbour thinks he's got magical qualities.'

'Maybe he has. People used to believe that about cats, didn't they, in medieval times? Thought they were associated with witches or something.'

I have no idea what witches are, little Charlie, or whether I'd want to be associated with them. All I knew was, I didn't particularly feel magical. But I *was*, after all, beginning to feel like I really could be the Cat Who Saved Christmas.

CHAPTER
TWENTY SIX

CHAPTER
TWENTY SIX

Those next few days, there was such a flurry of activity everywhere, I felt like wherever I went, people were tripping over me. Everyone in the village seemed to be shopping in a hurry, cooking in a hurry, wrapping things up in a hurry. And at the Big House it was even worse, with Julian and Laura and Harry rushing around putting up decorations and balloons and big tables and *another* big Christmas tree in the huge empty room they called the ballroom. I couldn't quite work out why it was called a ballroom when there wasn't a single ball in there to play with, but what did I know?

And then it was Christmas Eve, and everyone was even busier. The children were beside themselves with excitement. Almost every time Sarah opened her mouth it was to tell them that if they didn't calm down and behave themselves, Father Christmas wouldn't be coming. I tried to keep out of her way, as she ran around the kitchen with pots and pans, getting flustered and red in the face. But finally it was time to get ready for the party, and to my delight, Sarah told me I was invited too.

'You're one of the guests of honour,' she said, tying a piece of red Christmas ribbon round my neck, over my collar.

I normally hated wearing fussy things like that, but I was too excited about the party to care.

And then, just as everyone was getting their coats on ready to leave . . . George turned up.

I'm sure I don't have to tell you, do I, Charlie, how overjoyed I was! When I saw him come into the hallway I went a little bit crazy, walking round and round his legs, and rubbing my cheek against him madly to show him he still belonged to me. I know some cats treat their humans with disdain if they feel they've been neglected – walking away from them, twitching their tails – but I've never been able to hide my feelings like that. When George bent down and picked me up, I must have been the happiest cat in the world. I blinked so many kisses at him, I made my eyes hurt. Grace and Rose were shrieking with laughter at how loud I was purring.

'I'm sorry I haven't managed to get down here before now,' he was saying. 'I've been so busy in the new job. But I've brought all of you a few treats for Christmas, to make up for it – and another payment for Ollie's board and lodging of course, for you and next door.'

He put some bags of exciting-looking gift-wrapped parcels down on the table, then turned and looked at us all again – the children with their coats zipped up, me in my silly bow, Sarah with containers of food ready to take with us.

'Oh, I'm so sorry. You're just going out.'

'It's fine, George. Stay and have a coffee or something. There's no rush,' Martin said, giving a warning look to the children, who were shuffling their paws impatiently.

'Oh, *Daddy*,' little Rose said. 'Everyone will be there before us.'

'It's just a village party,' Sarah explained apologetically. 'A last-minute thing, actually.'

'Really? That's nice. Whose party?'

'You'll never believe it.' Sarah laughed. 'It's at the Big House. Julian Smythe has invited the whole village.'

'*Never!*'

'Yes!' She glanced at Martin and then added, 'Actually, George, why don't you join us? Nicky and Daniel next door are coming too – they'll be calling for us any minute now. We can tell you the whole story on the way there.'

'Oh, no. I couldn't. I haven't been invited.'

'Yes you have,' Martin said. 'You're part of the village – *everyone's* invited. We're all taking food with us. Come on, mate, it'll be great to have your company. Everyone'll be really chuffed to see you.'

So, together with Nicky and Daniel, we all set off up the hill. George even carried me the whole way – not because I couldn't walk, of course, but because I couldn't bear for him to put me down, even for a minute. I knew he'd soon be going back to London again and it might be a long time before he came back.

I can't tell you too much about the party, Charlie, except that the music was very noisy, all the children were very noisy, and lots of people seemed to be hugging each other and eating and drinking a lot. I'm afraid I put my paws over my ears and fell asleep on George's lap, and when I eventually woke up, I'd been put on a chair in a quiet corner of the hall, with one of the children's coats over me to keep me warm. I was happy to let George carry me home again.

I think it was quite late by the time the children had been tucked up in bed. This, by the way, was a longer process than usual, with strange rituals being carried out involving a glass of sherry and a mince pie being left on the fireplace, and stockings hung at the ends of both their beds, and a lot of giggling – none of which I could make any sense of. Then, after a last cup of coffee and chat with Sarah and Martin, George had to say goodbye to us all again. I went off to bed and tried not to cry. This time I felt a little more certain that he'd be back again.

When I woke up, it was quite obvious it was Christmas morning. The girls were shouting their heads off about the new toys they'd got, and next to my bed was a little red stocking full of cat treats, a catnip toy with jingly bells and feathers on, and a squeaky toy mouse.

'It's from George, Ollie,' Grace said when she came into the kitchen and saw me poking my nose into it. 'But we've bought you some presents too. They're under the tree. Happy Christmas!'

Dear George. And there was I, thinking Father Christmas must have been real after all.

Just after breakfast, a big car stopped outside Nicky and Daniel's house. I sat on Sarah's windowsill and watched as a male, a female and two quite large human kittens got out of the car carrying a lot of bags between them, and went in through the front door.

Sarah had been watching too. 'Nicky's parents and brothers are here,' she called out to Martin. 'Oh, I do hope it's all going to go smoothly for them.'

But of course, we had no idea whether it was going smoothly or roughly – not until much later, after everyone had opened more presents, eaten their Christmas dinner and pulled apart some really horrible things called *crackers*. They made a loud bang which sent me scuttling out to the kitchen and set the children off in fits of laughter. I really couldn't see what the point of that was.

It seemed a long day. They watched a lady called *Queen* on television, who did nothing but sit in a chair and talk, so I didn't know why it seemed so important, then they played games and ate chocolate, and later ate sandwiches and cake, and finally Grace and Rose looked like they were going to fall asleep where they sat, so they were packed off to bed.

I'd had my own dinner and was just thinking about going to settle down for the night, when there was a little light tap on the door, and Martin let in Nicky and Daniel, followed by their whole family. I immediately scarpered behind the sofa, anxious about the strange males.

'Oh, is this the cat you were telling us about?' one of the young males asked Nicky – and she laughed, and came to pick me up. She introduced me to everyone at the same time as introducing her family to Sarah and Martin.

'Ollie's our good luck cat,' Daniel said, quite seriously. 'All the good things that have happened recently – well, he seems to have been involved somehow.'

'We must get to know him, then,' the female said, giving me a little stroke. She seemed quite nice. I wondered what all the fuss had been about. 'And you, of course,' she added to Sarah and Martin. 'We've heard so much about you both. I understand from my daughter that you've been extremely kind to them since they moved in.'

'We're enjoying their friendship, that's all,' Sarah said.

'Well, I can't thank you enough for offering to put us up overnight like this. But we've brought some presents for your little girls, and a couple of bottles of wine.'

'You didn't have to do that,' Martin said. 'Please, sit down, everyone, and I'll get you all a drink. Have you had a good day together?'

'Yes. Definitely!' Nicky's mum smiled. 'We're thrilled to hear Nicky and Daniel's news, of course.'

Nicky was grinning like a Cheshire cat. Not that I've ever seen a Cheshire cat, Charlie, but apparently they grin, which is rather strange, as most cats can't.

'At first we were worried,' her dad said. 'I mean, they're so young, and, well, they haven't had a very good start, which was partly our fault.'

'No it wasn't, Dad,' Nicky said, but he held up a paw and went on:

'Yes. Our fault for not trusting the pair of you to make a go of it – not believing in you. To be honest, we didn't think it would last. We underestimated you both.'

'We're not out of the woods yet,' Daniel murmured.

'Maybe not, but we can see now that you're both doing your best, that you're committed to making it work. Perhaps it *is* a bit soon to be having the baby, but from what we've heard and seen today, if anybody can make a go of it, you two will. With Nicky's new job . . .'

'That's *such* a relief,' her mum said quietly to Sarah. 'I'd have been so worried at the thought of her travelling up to London every day with a tiny baby.'

'Yes. And Daniel getting all these recommendations for work in the field he was *always* cut out for – well, we can only hope things are going to steadily improve for you both now, and good for you. You deserve it.'

'They certainly do,' Sarah agreed.

'So, now we've seen how hard they're both working, and with the baby on the way – it's so exciting, our first grandchild,' the mum went on, 'the next step will be for them to buy a home of their own.'

Nicky and Daniel were beaming at each other.

'If we can find somewhere suitable – something small, of course, but with a little garden for when the baby's growing up – Mum and Dad are going to lend us the deposit,' Nicky said. 'Isn't that wonderful?'

Nicky's dad winked at Martin. 'We won't be expecting them to pay us back in a hurry. Perhaps when we're old and grey and we need help ourselves.'

'*And*,' Nicky's mum added, 'we're going to help them plan their wedding. If we'd realised they were only putting off getting married because they couldn't afford it, we'd have offered to help sooner.'

'We only want a quiet affair, Mum,' Nicky said. 'It won't have to cost the earth.'

'But you'll need a bit of help with the cost, whatever. And if we couldn't do that, for our only daughter, it'd be a poor show, wouldn't it.'

'Well,' Sarah said, raising her glass. 'I think this all definitely calls for a toast. To Nicky and Daniel – and the baby.' They all took a sip of their drinks. 'I hope you won't move too far away, though,' she added. 'We'd miss you.'

'No. We need to stay in the village. We've both got work here now,' Daniel said. 'Any idea if there are any houses for sale?'

'Oh!' Sarah suddenly sat up in her chair. 'Yes, of course, I do know of one. It's Barbara Griggs's cottage. You know she's moving in with Stan Middleton when they get married next month? The *For Sale* sign has only just gone up. It's not much bigger than your place next door, but there *are* two bedrooms, and yes, a little garden. And between you and me, it will need a bit of work. Just decorating, mainly.'

'I'd be happy to do that,' Daniel said immediately.

'I'd come over and help you,' Nicky's dad said. 'You'll be busy with your motor business.'

'I could give you a hand too,' Martin said.

'The point is, I suspect they'll take an offer, because it needs doing up. Why don't you see if you can go round and have a look after the holiday?' Sarah suggested.

'Oh, yes, we will, definitely. If we like it, it'd be perfect,' Nicky said. 'A bedroom for the baby. And a proper little garden.'

Everyone seemed so happy and excited, I didn't think they'd notice me creeping up to the little low table where Sarah had placed some very tempting dishes of snacks, including my favourite – little cubes of cheese. I stretched up with my two front paws on the table and was just about to grab a bit of cheese when the smaller one of the boys started giggling. Everyone looked round and to my embarrassment, I was caught in the act of trying to scamper off with the cheese in my mouth.

'Oh, Ollie!' Sarah laughed. At least she wasn't cross. 'I shouldn't have left all this food within your reach, should I? Are you hungry, boy? Or could you just not resist the cheese?'

'I think he's earned a few extra treats, don't you?' Martin said.

'Yes, I agree.' Daniel nodded, looking quite serious. He waited until Martin had got my food dish from the kitchen and started putting some cheese in it especially for me. 'Whatever you all say, I still believe Oliver's somehow helped turn things around for us,' he went on. 'I might have saved him from being stuck up the tree that day, but in return, it's like he's pretty much saved our lives.'

'Saved your *lives*? Exaggeration, or what, Daniel?' piped up the bigger of the two boys.

'All right,' Nicky said, 'let's put it this way – if nothing else, there's no denying he's certainly saved *Christmas* – for us, and probably for the whole village.'

'Definitely for young Caroline at the Big House,' Sarah added, and everyone murmured their agreement.

'So I'd like to suggest another toast,' Daniel said, topping up Nicky's glass with more lemonade. 'Here's to Oliver – our very special shared house guest. The Cat Who Saved Christmas!'

And they all raised their glasses, smiling at me, and joined in: 'To Oliver!' 'Here's to Oliver!'

If I'd been a human, I'd have been crying with happiness. But even if they *did* think I was very special, at the end of the day I'm still just a little cat. So I just finished my cheese, blinked kisses at them all and washed my whiskers before taking myself off to bed.

I'd done it, Charlie – they all said I had. Who'd have thought it? A little cat like me – after everything that had happened to me. I really was the Cat Who Saved Christmas.

EPILOGUE

EPILOGUE

Of course, the story doesn't end there, Charlie. Not quite.

Through all the freezing cold weather that came after Christmas, even when the snow came and I had to scamper through it with icy paws, I kept going back to the Big House to see Caroline. I saw her lovely golden fur grow back thick and shiny, her skinny little paws grow plumper and stronger, and her pale cheeks starting to turn a healthy pink. By the time the weather began to warm up again, she'd turned into a proper little girl, running around the house, laughing and shouting and playing with her friends. And with me.

But I'm getting ahead of myself now. Back at Sarah and Martin's house, something very important happened during those cold winter days. Their new kitten came home. The whole family went out together to collect her, and when they came back, Grace was carrying her very carefully in a cardboard box. Sarah closed all the doors and then they put the box down and let her out.

'Keep Ollie away for the first little while,' she told the children. 'We don't want her to be frightened.'

As if I, of all cats, was going to frighten a poor little kitten. I knew just how it felt to be tiny and defenceless in a scary new place. I sulked in my chair in the lounge, listening to the children's excited voices, imagining the little newcomer scurrying around the kitchen, wondering where she was, who these new humans were, and what had happened to her mother and her siblings. It brought back sad memories for me. But *this* new little kitten had come to a good home straight away. She was going to have a happy start in life.

Of course, she soon settled in, and quickly got used to me, too. I liked having her snuggle up with me in my bed. She was a bright little thing. Pretty soon she understood enough Cat for me to start giving her the benefit of my experience and teaching her about the human world. They called her Nancy. Apparently that was the name of someone in a book, a book about an Oliver.

'All we need now is an Artful Dodger,' Martin said. Sarah laughed, but I had no idea what he was talking about.

Not long after Nancy arrived, I was on one of my regular visits to Caroline when I heard a little squeaking noise coming from the kitchen. I sat up straight, ears erect and twitching. For a minute I thought Nancy must have followed me all the way there. I must have imagined it – it had sounded just like a kitten crying.

'Come and see, Oliver,' Caroline said, her eyes bright with excitement. 'Be very gentle, though.'

I followed her into the kitchen, across the wide stone floor, and there, by the big old cooker that seemed to be turned on, belting out heat all day every day throughout the winter, was a furry cat bed just like the one I had. And sitting in the middle of the bed, looking a bit lost, was a tiny kitten. He looked even smaller than Nancy, but it might have been because the bed was too big for him. And whereas you could already see Nancy was going to be a beauty, with her mother Suki's sleek shiny fur and creamy colouring, this little fellow looked like he'd been born with a cheeky expression on his face. He glanced up at me, his head on one side, one ear up and the other down, let out another little squeak and then clambered out of the bed, tripping over his own paws. He came right up to me, bold as brass, and began to rub his face against my legs. I couldn't believe it – it was like looking at a miniature version of my old friend. There was no doubt about it, he was quite clearly Tabby's son.

I couldn't help feeling fond of the little chap. He was certainly never going to lack for anything, this one – he'd fallen on his paws, all right, living in this beautiful house, with these lovely humans. But if he looked for a father figure, a good upright male cat to guide him as he grew up – well, Tabby certainly wasn't going to be around to do that. I made up my mind there and then that I'd take this little kitten under my own paw and tell him all he needed to know. Starting with my own life story, of course.

Yes, of course, that was you, Charlie – that was our first meeting. As you know, Nancy's your sister. Suki was your mother, and unfortunately for you, Tabby was your dad. I'm only joking, he's not a bad sort really. You could do worse than grow up like him, I suppose – you're already like him in so many ways.

Ever since that day, I've been coming back to see you, haven't I. Well, all right, I apologise – I know it's been a bit of a while this time. I've been a very busy cat. I've obviously had to spend time every day inspecting the rebuilding of my pub, and I'm happy to say that last week we moved back in. Yes – I'm back where I belong, with George, and if you'd ever been lost or homeless you'd understand why I'm so happy. And the thing is, you see, I still have to visit my friends at my two foster homes, because they keep telling me they miss me. And I need to do a tour of the village every day to make sure all my other human friends are getting along OK.

But look at you now! Have you had a couple of growth spurts since we last met? You must be almost fully grown by now. I'll certainly never be able to call you *Little Kitten* again. You do realise you'll probably end up growing bigger than me, don't you? You're quite the young man about town now, I suppose. And with that cheeky way about you, I daresay you'll be getting all the female cats' hearts racing, just like that old rascal Tabby still seems to do. But I hope you'll always remember what a lucky cat you are, to be living here. It was always a cat's paradise, with those huge grounds and these big rooms to run around in, but everything's so much nicer here now that Laura's finished furnishing it and making it really homely. Julian's a good, kind male – who'd have guessed how much he actually does like cats, after all. And of course, you love Caroline, don't you. Everyone says how quickly she got better after you came to live with her.

Where are they, by the way? In the sitting room? Come on, then, let's go and see them.

*

Ah, just look at them! Do they do that all the time? Sitting snuggled up together on the sofa like two cats curled up in their basket? Why do they keep looking at each other and grinning like that? To think, I used to wonder whether Laura had something wrong with her when she said she liked Julian. I'm glad she's moved in. It's nice to see them so happy together, isn't it – nice for Caroline, too.

Caroline's pleased to see us – look, she's coming over to play with us now.

Hello, Caroline. Ha! It still makes you laugh when I rub myself around your legs like this, doesn't it. Sorry if it tickles, but I just can't help it – it's so lovely to see you up on your two back paws all the time. Yes, I've come to talk to Charlie, but I'm here to see *you* as well. You say you're excited about Christmas?

Surely it's not going to be another Christmas again, so soon? It'll be your first one, Charlie. Now, remember what I told you about the Christmas tree. You're going to want to play with those baubles. They're irresistible. You might have to sit on your paws to stop yourself. You say they're bringing the tree in tomorrow? You saw Harry chopping it down outside? Oh, listen – they're just talking about it now.

'I don't mind where we put it, Julian,' Laura says. 'In here, or in the ballroom. You decide.'

'I don't mind either,' he says, looking back into her eyes with that silly smile. 'I want everything the way *you'd* like it this Christmas, darling. No expense spared. Decorations everywhere. We're celebrating Caroline's recovery – and us all being together.'

And look who else is here! It's Nicky, with baby Benjamin. He's getting big now. Do you like him, Charlie? Yes, I know he makes a lot of squealing and squawking noises, but he can't help that, you used to do it yourself.

It's nice that Nicky has come to visit Caroline, with the baby. Look how Caroline enjoys fussing over him. Nicky's put him down on the carpet so she can play with him. So she often comes here when she's not looking after Freya and Henry? Ah, I see – she's got friendly with Laura. They like to have a chat together. It looks like Julian's going to leave them alone to talk. Perhaps he's going off to do some *Saturday pottering* like Martin does.

'How's the house coming on, Nicky?' Laura's asking her now.

'Slowly!' She laughs. 'But we're getting there. We're going to put a new kitchen in after Christmas – we've been saving up, and Dad's going to help. Daniel's so busy with the car repair business.'

'I hear he's going part-time at the shop in London now?'

'Yes. He's hoping to give it up altogether eventually. He's got dreams of having his own workshop one day, and employing an apprentice.' She gives another little laugh. 'Good to have dreams, I suppose.'

'I hope they come true. For both of you,' Laura says, squeezing Nicky's hand. 'It's good to see you looking so happy.'

'And you,' Nicky says. 'I'm so glad it's going well, Laura. Julian's a good man.'

'Yes.' Laura's cheeks go pink and she's smiling to herself. 'It's going to be a wonderful Christmas. He's determined to make everything perfect. For Caroline – for all of us. A celebration. It's been a good year.'

'Yes, it has,' Nicky agrees. 'Who'd have thought, this time last year, that Daniel and I would be married and living in our own home with our baby by now? It's been a really special year.'

'For me, too,' I meow at them, in case they'd forgotten me – and they both turn and smile.

'He always looks as if he's trying to tell us something,' Laura says. 'I wish I knew what he was thinking.'

It just doesn't seem to occur to them, you see, Charlie? If they'd only put themselves out a bit, and learn to speak some Cat! But however much they love us, and care for us and try to understand us, as far as I know not a single human has ever done it. Never mind, you'll just have to do what we all do – listen to their conversations in Human and let them think there's something unusual about you because you can understand them. One day, you might even have an important job yourself, like me – saving Christmas . . . or something else . . . for your humans. If not in this life – maybe in one of the other eight. Who knows? That may not be a myth, after all.

ACKNOWLEDGEMENTS

With thanks to Emily Yau and Gillian Green at Ebury Press for entrusting me with the writing of this story, and especially for Emily's support and encouragement throughout the book's development.